Tanner Jones

His eyes were even bluer than in his picture, Dori noticed. When she'd first seen his ad in *Texas Men,* she'd thought he was gorgeous. Now she realized the ad hadn't done him justice. Six feet tall, with unruly sun-streaked hair and a whipcord-lean body, Tanner was the hero Dori had been waiting for....

He turned his gaze in her direction and heat filtered through her. She imagined candlelit evenings and rumpled bedsheets...and the two of them in each other's arms.

Tanner didn't say a word, but seemed to know what she was thinking. A bold grin split his handsome face.

"As I live and breathe, if it ain't the famous Tanner Jones."

The comment was a rude awakening. Dori turned and saw her ex-husband sitting on a stool by the counter. *It was great while it lasted.* Well, now she knew how her relationship with Tanner would work out. Jimmy Jr., would scare him away, as surely as he had all the others.

So much for her hero....

Dear Reader,

In one of my favorite "Cathy" cartoons, Cathy claims to be ready for marriage, so her friend Andrea offers to set her up with a blind date. Cathy replies, "Ack! I'm ready for marriage, not *dating!*"

I think Cathy would love the concept of a mail-order catalog filled with men ready to commit. It takes all the guesswork out of it. What could be more of a turn-on than pages of gorgeous hunks, each one searching for that special someone? Talk about your ultimate home shopping guide!

When my heroine, Dori Fitzpatrick, opens a copy of *Texas Men* and glimpses a picture of Tanner Jones clad in a muscle shirt and a hard hat, she melts like a pat of butter on an Abilene sidewalk. The confidence in those intense blue eyes convinces her that at last she's found her hero, the man who will put her life back to rights again. Best of all, he's looking for someone just like her.

I suspect you'll fall in love with Tanner right along with Dori. I certainly did.

Happy reading!

Vicki Lewis Thompson

Vicki Lewis Thompson
HOLDING OUT FOR A HERO

Harlequin Books

TORONTO • NEW YORK • LONDON
AMSTERDAM • PARIS • SYDNEY • HAMBURG
STOCKHOLM • ATHENS • TOKYO • MILAN
MADRID • WARSAW • BUDAPEST • AUCKLAND

For Ralfanita Overton Forman, a belated thank-you for
befriending this city girl thirty-five years ago.

ISBN 0-373-25700-7

HOLDING OUT FOR A HERO

Copyright © 1996 by Vicki Lewis Thompson.

This edition published by arrangement with Harlequin Books S.A.

Printed in U.S.A.

1

FOR THE HUNDREDTH TIME, Dori Fitzpatrick checked the wall clock. Twenty minutes to go. At exactly 9:00 p.m., Tanner Jones would walk through the door of the Double Nickel Truck Stop and Café with the power to change her life.

Nearly all Dori's customers knew about her date with Tanner and understood the significance of it. But nobody had brought up the subject, which only increased her nervousness. Maybe if she brought it up, her system would settle down a little.

"The best thing about Tanner is that he's not rich," she announced as she moved down the red Formica counter, topping off coffee cups. She'd known most of these truckers for years and they expected a bottomless cup when they sat at her counter. It didn't matter to them that she was about to have her life transformed on this Sunday evening in the West Texas town of Los Lobos.

Heck Tyrrell adjusted his Peterbilt gimme cap. "Just sayin' he ain't rich ain't sayin' much, Dori."

"It most certainly is." Dori emptied the pot and measured fragrant grounds into the basket for a fresh brew. "I wouldn't marry a rich man again if he made love like an angel and looked like Mel Gibson."

"Not everybody with money is like Jimmy Jr.," said the man sitting next to Heck. Travis Neff, a veteran trucker, had given Dori her first tip years ago when she'd started working at the café as a teenager.

Dori started the coffee trickling into the pot, then turned back to Heck and Travis. "Maybe not, but I don't care to take the chance. No rich man will run my life ever again."

Heck set down his cup. "But I sure think you're making a big mistake, taking up with some ol' boy who put his picture in a magazine just to attract women. What kinda person would do that?"

Dori opened her mouth to reply.

"Number five's up," called the cook as he shoved an order of pork chops, mashed potatoes and gravy onto the pass-through from the kitchen.

"That'd be mine," said Travis. He loved to eat and it showed. "For once I agree with Heck," he said. "I don't like the idea of you setting up a date with some stranger from East Texas."

"We've written several letters back and forth." Dori set the steaming plate in front of Travis along with side dishes of applesauce, coleslaw and a basket of rolls. "I don't think of him as a stranger."

"Letters," Travis said with a dismissive shrug as he picked up his fork. "Anybody can write letters. Isn't he from around Dallas somewhere? Those big-city boys are slick as hog fat, Dori. He could have a police record or be one of them left-wingers. He could be—" Travis paused and his round face turned pink "—one of them kinky types . . . you know what I mean."

Dori took a box from underneath the counter and started restocking sugar packets. "He's a construction worker, and his letters don't sound kinky at all. Besides,

I've told y'all why I wrote in to the magazine. Nobody in this town will ask me out, let alone consider something more serious, and that's the plain fact of it, Travis."

"Bunch of lily-livered pansies," Travis muttered into his plate.

"Easy for you to say. You're married," Heck replied in a low voice, glancing around to see who might be listening. Almost every one of the men sitting on counter stools was intent on the conversation, not to mention several others gathered in the café's four booths. A good portion of them drove for Devaney Trucking, the town's chief industry.

"Aw, hell," Heck said in a more normal voice. "Might as well get it out in the open. There's lots of guys in this room who would take you out in a heartbeat, if they didn't think they'd suffer the consequences." He gave a half turn on his stool to survey the room. "Am I right?" The room was silent except for Waylon Jennings crooning from the jukebox.

Dori didn't need to look into the faces of the single men in the restaurant to see every man jack of them was embarrassed by the truth of what Heck had said. She cleared an empty plate from the counter and swept up crumbs with a damp rag as she talked. "Hey, I don't expect anybody to risk his job by crossing the Devaneys. I know good and well Jimmy Jr. has threatened to fire or blackball any driver who so much as buys me an ice-cream cone. I wouldn't *let* any of y'all take that chance. That's why I decided to try this magazine thing."

Travis put down his fork. "Let me take a look at that magazine one more time."

Dori rinsed her cleaning rag in the sink and dried her hands before reaching under the counter for her copy of *Texas Men*, which she'd folded back permanently to the picture of Tanner Jones, East Texas construction worker. Beneath his hard hat shone the bluest eyes she'd ever seen. Tanner Jones wouldn't be so tough to sit across from at the breakfast table every morning, she thought, her heartbeat quickening.

"Don't be getting any gravy on it," she warned as she handed it to Travis. "This picture may turn out to be an heirloom for my children and grandchildren."

The whole counter full of men snorted at that, but she faced them down. "Y'all know that nine is my lucky number. Tanner's bachelor number nine in the magazine. And as if that's not enough, that's the September issue, and I picked it up on September the ninth."

"And you asked him to meet you here at nine tonight." Travis sounded pleased with himself that he'd made the connection. "How come you didn't make it for October ninth?"

"I wanted to, but it didn't fall right, with my day off being Monday. I didn't want to have to come in to work the first day he's in town."

Heck shook his head. "You're way too superstitious, Dori Mae Fitzpatrick."

"Ha." She took a piece of pie out of a clear plastic display case and brought it to one of the truckers who'd signaled to her. She remembered his favorite was apple and he smiled when she brought the right flavor. "I happen to know, Heck Tyrrell, that you have a rabbit's foot dangling from the rearview mirror of your cab. Don't go telling me who's superstitious."

A trucker spoke up from the end of the counter. "I've got a lucky silver dollar from Vegas. I take that dang thing pretty near everywhere I go. Leave Dori alone about her lucky number, Heck. Everybody's got something like that."

"Yeah," Heck grumbled, "but Dori's fixing to spend her life with some ol' boy because he happened to be the ninth bachelor in a matchmaking magazine."

"I am not!" Dori moved around the counter as she added up a ticket for booth number three and placed it facedown on the table. "This first date is just a look-see," she continued, glancing at the clock again. Ten minutes to go. "Don't worry, I'll put Tanner Jones through his paces. And of course, he has to be good with kids, so I'm trying him out right away on Little Jim. Tomorrow the three of us are going into Abilene."

"How's that little cowpoke doing?" Travis asked, munching a roll.

"I just picked up some new pictures." Dori scanned her customers and made sure everyone had what they needed before she reached beneath the counter again and came up with a packet of snapshots. "Last Monday I took him to Abilene Lake. We got a little sunburned, but it was great." She handed the packet to Travis and noticed the men from booth three coming up to the cash register. "Excuse me a minute, Travis."

Dori rang up the bill and delivered her standard, "Y'all come back," before returning to where Travis and Heck were going through her twenty-four snapshots. "Isn't he the handsomest boy in the world?"

"Good-lookin' tadpole," Heck agreed. "Where'd all that red hair come from?"

"My side." Dori touched her brunette hair that was caught back in a net for work. "I have some red highlights, but my grandmother was a flaming redhead. And Little Jim has the spirit to go with that hair!" Dori laughed. Just thinking about her son put her in a good mood. "He has a mind of his own, all right. Those kindergarten teachers better be ready for some surprises when he shows up next fall."

"He'll be in school already?" Travis handed the pictures back to her. "Seems like he was born just last month."

"That's how it is with kids," Dori said. "I'm sure your two were like that. Babies one day, all grown up the next. I just wish..." She didn't finish the sentence. Travis, Heck and many of the men at the counter knew what Dori wished. Jimmy Jr. had taken Dori to court soon after the divorce and obtained custody on the grounds that Dori had to work and put the toddler in day care.

If she'd insisted on a bigger settlement at the time of the divorce, she wouldn't have had to hire someone to watch Little Jim. Her pride had essentially robbed her of her beloved son. Friends had advised her that one reasonable way to get him back was to remarry and prove to the judge that a two-parent household was a healthier environment for Little Jim. Tanner Jones was due in six minutes.

"Say, Dori, sweetheart, what's the chance of getting a cup of coffee down at this end of the counter?"

Dori tensed at the sound of the familiar voice and looked down the length of the counter straight into Jimmy Jr.'s green eyes.

Jimmy lounged on a stool, his Stetson at a rakish angle. His blond good looks were the sort to turn women's heads, and they'd turned hers at the age of eighteen. But she'd outgrown Jimmy Jr. Her hands balled into fists. She should have guessed he'd show up tonight.

"Heard you had some East Texas stud coming in at nine," Jimmy said. "Thought I'd take a look at him."

AS HE CRUISED WEST on Interstate 20 past cotton fields and bobbing oil rigs, Tanner Jones caught the fragrance of the single rose he'd picked up in Abilene. The scent cut through a slight gas smell that told him the engine needed tuning. Considering the odometer read more than a hundred and fifty thousand miles, he was lucky the truck hadn't broken down between here and Dallas. He hadn't thought of that when he'd borrowed one of his employees' pickups to make this trip. There were a lot of things he probably hadn't thought of.

Clothes hadn't been a problem. He'd packed his most worn, comfortable jeans and Western shirts and left the custom-made suits in the closet. He preferred the old clothes, anyway. Sometimes he wondered if he'd be happier living the life of a construction worker. But then he'd have to work for someone else, and he'd never been very good at that.

His independence had paid off, and he'd become one of the richest home builders in East Texas. But recently, it seemed that every woman he'd dated was only attracted to his money. Now that he'd achieved financial security he longed for the basics his parents enjoyed—a cheerful home, a loving mate, children. Ironically, money seemed to be getting in his way.

So here he was driving an old truck to Los Lobos while his shiny new Dodge Ram sat in the garage. The man Dori Fitzpatrick would meet tonight was the real Tanner Jones, he told himself. There was nothing wrong with disguising his wealth to see if a woman could fall in love with him for himself alone. That had been his plan from the moment he'd agreed to appear in *Texas Men*. Nothing in the profile was untrue—just incomplete—and the picture could have been taken on any day he visited one of his construction sites.

But when creating his plan he hadn't figured on battling his honest streak, which ran through him a mile wide, apparently. He pacified his conscience by thinking about how thrilled Dori would be when she eventually found out he was rich. No doubt she'd forgive the white lie.

As the miles ticked off, Tanner looked for the Los Lobos exit. Dori had instructed him to drive through town to the far side until he saw the Double Nickel Truck Stop and Café. She said he could come in on the second exit and miss the town's main street, but she thought he should get a look at where she lived. He was willing to follow her lead, so he flipped on his turn signal at the first exit for Los Lobos, marked Business Loop.

The town limit sign recorded a population of 8,857. Just beyond that, Tanner noticed a huge sign at the fenced entryway to a large lot full of identically painted eighteen-wheeler cabs. The sign read Devaney Trucking. Must be a gold mine, he thought. Positioned on I-20 not far from the intersection of Highway 84, the company was well placed in Texas and nearly dead center between the Atlantic and Pacific coasts. Tanner bet the Devaneys pretty much ran the town of Los Lobos.

He drove past the Prairie Schooner Motel and RV Park where he had reservations for the next week, then on down the main street. The shopping basics were represented—hardware store, bank, post office, clothing store, hair salon—but Tanner figured most people drove to Abilene for major purchases. That's where he'd take Dori for a nice dinner one night, and maybe even some live theater. If nothing looked good to him in Abilene, he could always charter a plane and... Tanner blinked and cursed softly in the darkness. He had to stop thinking like a rich man. The first time he forgot and pulled out a gold card, the ruse would be over.

Then he began to wonder if he remembered how to court a woman without expensive dinners and extravagant gifts. Maybe this wouldn't be quite as easy as he'd imagined. He glanced at his watch and realized it looked far too expensive for the image he was trying to give. After checking the time he took it off and shoved it in the glove compartment.

Dori had agreed to meet him at nine—no sooner and no later. She'd been very specific about that and had even confessed she'd written to him in the first place because he was the ninth bachelor in the September issue of the magazine. He hoped she wasn't too hung up on superstition.

Hell, this whole thing was crazy. They'd probably hate each other on sight. Maybe she'd been entranced by the hard hat and wouldn't care for the way he looked in a worn black Stetson. And what would he talk about? He couldn't describe his work without getting into trouble, and work had been his whole life for the past ten years. He didn't know if he could make conversation about much else.

As for Dori, she might have all sorts of irritating habits. She might not look anything like her picture, and he was basing a lot on that photograph. Her beauty had captured his attention first, but he'd received lots of pictures of good-looking women in the past few weeks. He'd had no way of knowing if the photos were recent or even legitimate. One woman had sent in a magazine clipping of a rising movie star and had claimed to look "just like her."

But Dori's picture had seemed right to him. Especially her eyes, which were a vulnerable soft brown with a touch of sadness and a hint of smoky passion lurking in their depths.

Tanner chuckled and shook his head. What a romantic he was. The expression he'd read as a mixture of sorrow and passion was probably nearsightedness. And all those letters she'd written about loving sunsets more than diamonds, and moonlight more than pearls, might be something she'd copied from a book, not something she truly believed.

Neon glowed up ahead on the right side of the road, and he made out the words Double Nickel. Rows of canopied gas pumps dwarfed the small building housing the café. Several big rigs were parked nearby, along with a few cowboy Cadillacs—fancy pickups with plenty of chrome gleaming in the lights from the parking lot. Tanner's stomach clenched as he realized Dori was inside that cozy little building waiting for him. He could still turn around and forget the whole thing. But he flipped on the right-turn signal. He'd come this far. He might as well see it through.

DORI WEIGHED HER OPTIONS. Technically, she couldn't deny Jimmy Jr. service in the Double Nickel unless he became obnoxious. She removed a cup and saucer from a stack on the drain board, poured Jimmy's coffee and carried it to him, along with a handful of creamer containers. Jimmy would wail about needing more cream in his coffee if she didn't.

Jimmy pushed back his hat with his thumb and winked at her. "Thanks, darlin'."

She looked him in the eye. "If you make trouble with Tanner Jones, I'll call Deputy Holt. So help me, I will."

Jimmy shrugged and glanced down the counter to where Travis Neff still held the issue of *Texas Men.* "Whatcha got there, Travis?"

"This here belongs to Dori." Travis held it out to her.

Dori started down the counter to retrieve her magazine, but Jimmy caught her wrist. "I think I'll have me a piece of pie, too, Dori. Would you get that for me? You know the kind I like."

Dori trembled with fury. "Let go of me."

"Oh." Jimmy looked down at his fingers encircling her wrist. "Force of habit, darlin'." He didn't release her, and his thumb caressed her pulse. "While I'm eating my pie, I'll take a look at that magazine, Travis."

Dori glanced at Travis, who appeared ready to resist. And if he did, he'd no longer be working for Devaney Trucking come morning. Travis had a wife, and kids in college. It was just a magazine, Dori reasoned, not worth having a man lose his job over. She swallowed. "He's welcome to see it, Travis."

Travis looked unhappy but relieved. As he passed the magazine down the counter, Jimmy released Dori's wrist and reached for it. Dori turned toward the pie keeper and pulled out the last piece of lemon meringue. *Someday,* she vowed. But when she made her stand against Jimmy Jr., she wouldn't risk the welfare of innocent bystanders.

"So this is the ol' boy I've been hearing about for days." Jimmy held the magazine at arm's length and squinted at the picture of Tanner. "He don't look so tough to me."

Dori clenched her fists. "Jimmy, I'm warning you . . ."

"Hey, relax, baby." Jimmy set the magazine beside his pie plate. "I ain't fixin' to do a single thing except look him over, just like everybody else packed in here. This is the most excitin' thing happening in town tonight."

Dori sighed. She had herself to blame for this mess. Meeting Tanner in such a public place and telling people about it was bound to stir up curiosity. But she'd done it for her own protection. Despite Tanner's wonderful letters, he could be some weirdo. Even the publishers of the magazine warned their women readers to use caution until they got to know the bachelor they'd decided to contact.

Pulling her order pad from her pocket, she wrote out Jimmy's ticket. She wanted to slap it on the counter, but she laid it down carefully and walked away. It was almost nine, and Alice had just come in the door to relieve her.

"Now see what I've done," Jimmy said. "I'm powerful sorry, Dori Mae. I spilled coffee all over your Romeo's face."

Dori had known it would happen the moment she'd given up the fight for the magazine. She could probably order another, if she wanted it as a keepsake. While she waited for Alice to put her purse away in the back and come out to take over, Dori pointedly ignored Jimmy as she finished cleaning up and pocketing her tips. An uneasy silence had fallen over the men sitting at the counter, but none of them made a move to leave.

"I'll find a way to get rid of him," Jimmy said, obviously trying to goad her into a response.

She glanced up at Jimmy and fought the urge to scream that she was never coming back to him, so he might as well get on with his life. But he wouldn't have believed her. He'd bragged to his friends, who had passed on the word to her, that eventually she'd come crawling back, love starved and desperate to be with her son again.

And the truth was that she *was* desperate—longing to greet her son every morning when he awoke and kiss him every night before he went to sleep. And sometimes she desperately craved the comfort—and yes, the excitement—of a man's strong arms. But Jimmy Jr. was not that man.

"I'll discourage him in no time. See if I don't," Jimmy said.

Dori lifted her chin. "Maybe he's the kind who won't discourage so easy."

Then a man walked through the door at exactly nine o'clock. Dori noticed that his eyes were even bluer than in his picture. Tanner Jones had arrived.

2

MINUS THE ROSE, which he'd lost the nerve to take with him into a café full of truckers, Tanner pushed open the door of the Double Nickel. Just inside the entrance he paused to get his bearings and saw Dori at once. After that, he could see no one else.

Her picture hadn't done her justice. Her skin was more translucent, her eyes more luminous, than a mere camera could reveal. She noticed him as quickly as he'd noticed her and she became absolutely still, mirroring his absorption. For a few seconds they just looked at each other. Tanner knew it was the sort of crystallized moment that would live forever in his memory, no matter how things turned out.

"As I live and breathe, if it ain't the famous Tanner Jones."

The comment snapped through Tanner's preoccupation like a whiplash. If someone in this cafe had already recognized him as the owner of Jones Construction, his plan was dead. He glanced warily at the cowboy standing about three feet from him, his hat tilted back and a mocking smile on his handsome face. All conversation in the café had stopped.

"You fooled me at first," the cowboy said into the strained silence. "I thought maybe you'd wear your hard hat and muscle shirt."

Tanner relaxed a little. The guy probably recognized him from the article in *Texas Men*. And for some reason, he was threatened by Tanner's arrival. Tanner shifted his weight to the balls of his feet so he could side-step a punch if one came. From the gleam in the guy's eyes, Tanner almost expected it might.

Instead, the cowboy stuck out his hand. "Let me be the first to welcome you to Los Lobos, Mr. Tanner Jones." His exaggerated courtesy reeked of sarcasm. "I'm Jimmy Devaney, Jr., Dori's husband."

Husband. Tanner had wondered what little glitch would pop up to spoil his fantasy of Dori as the perfect woman for him, but this sure as hell hadn't been one he'd expected. He could have sworn Dori had written that she was divorced. Not separated, or thinking of leaving her husband, but divorced.

Then Tanner registered the last name this cowboy had just given him. Devaney. As in Devaney Trucking, the biggest business in town. Wonderful. He shook Jimmy Devaney's hand. "Didn't know Dori was married," he said quietly.

"I'm not. We've been divorced for two years." Her voice had a lazy drawl that he liked, but there was a strong current of tension running beneath her words. She approached him with a small purse slung over her shoulder, bringing with her the scent of fresh flowers. Her cheeks were pink and the dreaminess he'd seen in her deep brown eyes when he'd first walked in had been replaced with anger.

She inserted herself between Tanner and Jimmy Devaney, with her back to Jimmy. Then she took an unsteady breath and managed a smile as she looked up at

Tanner. "I'm Dori Fitzpatrick. I'm happy to meet you, Tanner."

Her smile made him forget all about her ex-husband. It was the most uncomplicated, honest smile he'd seen on a woman in years. He touched the brim of his hat. "I'm happy to meet you, too, Dori."

She gestured toward an empty booth. "How about a cup of coffee?"

"Sounds great."

As he started to take her elbow to guide her in that direction, Devaney grabbed his arm. Tanner released Dori's elbow and shook off Devaney's grasp. Then he turned slowly to face him. "What's your problem, mister?"

Devaney glared at him. "I'd advise you to keep your hands off my wife."

"Dori tells me you're divorced." Tanner kept his voice even. "That makes her your ex-wife, cowboy."

"Dori's the mother of my kid. And I aim to see she don't disgrace him by acting like a little tramp."

Tanner's jaw tightened. "Now that's a real ugly thing to say about a lady, Devaney. I advise you to apologize."

"Apologize?" Devaney waved something in his left hand and Tanner recognized a coffee-stained copy of *Texas Men*. "When she goes and writes to a total stranger and asks him for a date? Where I come from, there's a name for a woman who'd do that!"

Tanner sighed. He was going to have to fight the guy now. "Okay, Devaney," he said, his voice echoing the weariness he felt at the prospect of a fistfight in the parking lot of the Double Nickel Truck Stop and Café. "You win. Let's go settle this outside."

Devaney's jaw worked and he clenched his hands, but he didn't move. "You'd like that, wouldn't you?"

"No, but I thought you could hardly wait."

Dori came up beside Tanner. "You're not going to fight him. I can't let you do that."

"How sweet." Devaney sneered as he glanced around the café. "She's worried about him. Anybody think I should dirty my hands on a drifter from East Texas? Hell, I could buy and sell you twenty times over, Jones."

"If you say so." Tanner now understood the glitch he'd been expecting. If he wanted Dori Fitzpatrick, he'd have to get past this moron, who was unfortunately connected to the most powerful family in town. Tanner figured anybody with a lick of sense would make his excuses and start the long drive back to Dallas. Hell, he was still getting responses from that article in *Texas Men.* Somebody else would turn up, somebody without a belligerent ex-husband in the wings.

"And I got important contacts," Devaney added.

"I'm sure you do." Tanner was sick of the prolonged exchange, but at least it confirmed what he'd suspected. Like most bullies, Devaney was a coward. There would be no fight in the parking lot, at least not until Devaney had rounded up a few of his friends to safeguard the outcome and make sure the attack caught Tanner unprepared. "Tell you what, let's table this discussion for now," Tanner said.

"Table it?" Devaney sneered. "What are you, some chairman of the board?"

Dammit. Tanner sucked in a breath. "Just an expression," he said quickly. "We're both tired. Let's discuss this later."

Devaney pulled his hat over his eyes. "Nothin' more to discuss, sucker. Here's the deal." He pointed a finger at Tanner. "Get too friendly with Dori and I'll make your life so miserable you'll wish you'd never set foot in Los Lobos." He stormed out of the café without a backward glance.

The truckers sitting in the café muttered under their breaths. Then they gradually returned to their meals and conversations.

Dori touched Tanner's arm. "Forget the coffee. I should have known this wouldn't work."

Readying his excuses about why he needed to get back to Dallas, Tanner faced her.

"I'm sorry I made you drive all this way for nothing," she said. The light had died in her brown eyes. "I'll be happy to pay for your motel room and gas, though."

The memory of how excited she'd looked when he'd walked in the door came back to haunt him. He felt his resolve to leave being replaced with a desire to bring back that glow of anticipation. He fought that desire with images of himself beaten to a bloody pulp by Devaney's friends. In a town run by Devaneys, nobody would come to the aid of a stranger from East Texas.

"Look, I understand completely," Dori said. "There's no point in taking on somebody like Jimmy Jr. when there's no reason to."

Ah, but there was. He'd begun to fall in love, just a little, while reading and rereading her letters and gazing at her picture. In person she was even more beautiful, with a sweetly curved body and dewy skin that beckoned for his touch. He searched her expression. "Do you want me to leave?"

A sad smile appeared. "That's not a fair question."

The sad smile did it. The last of his good sense evaporated in its gentle warmth. "Let's have coffee," he said. Then he watched the glimmer of hope in her eyes grow and discovered it gave him far too much pleasure. He was in big trouble.

"I guess I owe you at least a cup of coffee," she said, as if she dared not read too much into his suggestion.

"At least that much." Tanner settled across from her in the booth and watched in fascination as she removed the net from her hair. Red-brown tresses the color of polished walnut tumbled over her shoulders and caught the light. She raised a hand and signaled the waitress behind the counter with a grace that captivated him. No wonder Jimmy Devaney, Jr., wanted her back, Tanner thought. Her equal wouldn't exist within a five-hundred-mile radius of this tiny burg.

"Are you hungry?" Dori asked as the waitress approached. "I get a discount here, so order anything you want."

"Coffee's fine," he said.

She looked disappointed.

"Maybe a piece of pie," he added, ridiculously willing to please her. "Apple, if they have it."

Dori smiled at the waitress. "Two cups of coffee, Alice, and a piece of apple pie for Mr. Jones." She glanced at him. "Warm, with ice cream?"

"Sure." He loved the way Dori said "ice," as if it were spelled "ahce." Tanner had grown up in the Midwest, and although he'd lived in East Texas for fifteen years, he'd never picked up a Texas drawl.

Alice wrote the order on her ticket pad. "Cream in your coffee, Mr. Jones?" She studied him closely.

"Black, thanks."

"Good." Alice left with a satisfied expression on her face.

"What's good about black coffee?" Tanner asked Dori.

"Jimmy Jr. drinks it with a ton of cream."

"Oh." It wasn't much, but at least here was a little evidence that somebody wanted Dori to find a new love. He wasn't sure how Alice would stack up in a back-alley brawl, though. Then he remembered the rose sitting on the seat of his truck. Now might be just the right moment to get it. "Would you excuse me a minute?" he asked. "I left something in the truck."

She looked startled, then suspicious. "Uh, sure. I'll, ah, be here."

As he headed out the door, he realized she thought he was never coming back. Well, now was as good a time as any for her to learn that her ex-husband might be a coward, but Tanner Jones didn't operate that way.

DORI WATCHED HIM walk out and berated herself for being surprised. Of course he was leaving. He'd just been waiting for a convenient moment, and her intuition about his strength of character had only been wishful thinking. A soggy blanket of despair settled over her. Until his unimaginative exit just now, she'd liked everything about him, from his startling blue eyes to his scuffed Western boots. She'd liked the way he'd been willing to step outside with Jimmy, although she never would have allowed that to happen. He hadn't seemed like the kind to sneak out of a thorny situation, but that's exactly what he'd done with some lame excuse about getting something from his truck.

Damn, she just might cry. Grabbing a napkin from the metal holder, she pressed it against her eyes and lowered her head while she thought of the one subject that usually kept her spirits up. But even the mental image of Little Jim didn't help much tonight, because now she wondered if she'd ever live in the same house with her child again.

"It's a little wilted, but still pretty," explained a deep baritone near her shoulder.

She sniffed and glanced up into the concerned blue depths of Tanner's eyes. Then her gaze drifted to the deep red rose he held toward her. She looked away quickly and bit her trembling lip as tears quivered on her eyelashes.

"Hey, Dori," he murmured, easing in next to her on the seat and covering her hand with his.

His thigh rested next to hers and the hand holding the rose lay over the back of the booth. The scent of deep, piney woods enveloped her, and she had an almost uncontrollable urge to nestle into the curve of his arm, to soak up his solid strength.

"You thought I was leaving."

She nodded, still not trusting herself to look at him.

He rubbed his fingers across the hollows between her knuckles. "I knew you thought that. I could see it in your eyes when I told you I had to get something out of the truck. Even if I'd have reassured you, you wouldn't have believed me."

His easy caress was the most gentle, loving touch she'd experienced in months. She'd suspected how needy she was, but hadn't understood the depth of it. With almost no effort, he was transforming her wariness into a languorous anticipation for anything he suggested. As she reacted to his touch, she began to worry that her objectivity would disappear in no time, and she had to remain objective. So much was at stake.

She took a deep breath and pulled her hand from beneath his. Then she angled herself to face him, but moved to the far corner of the booth. He watched her with compelling intensity. A tightening of sensual awareness told her she would have to be very careful. She didn't plan to become physically involved with this man until she knew a great deal more about him, but restraining herself wouldn't be easy—not when he could churn her up so completely with just a look.

When he smiled and held out the rose, her breath caught in her throat. There was more tenderness in that one smile than Jimmy Jr. had shown her in the entire seven years of their marriage. And as she absorbed it, she realized she couldn't let this obviously nice guy stay and be subjected to whatever Jimmy might dish out.

She accepted the rose. "I will remember this night, and your gallantry, for the rest of my life," she said softly. She lowered her lashes and buried her nose in the fragrant petals for a long, heady moment before lifting her gaze to his once more. "But I want you to go. I wasn't honest about the situation here, and I've lured you into a trap because I needed . . ."

"A hero? A knight in shining armor?"

"Something like that. It was selfish to ask you to come in and slay these dragons for me. I'm sure you had dozens of answers to that article in *Texas Men*."

"Nope. Just yours." His eyes twinkled.

"You folks ready for that pie and coffee now?"

Dori glanced up at Alice, who stood patiently balancing a tray holding two coffees and apple pie à la mode. Dori blushed with embarrassment. She'd forgotten all about the order, which Alice must have held in the kitchen while she waited for the most diplomatic moment to deliver it. The truckers had probably been watching the whole scene between Dori and her new beau with great interest, too.

"Certainly," Dori said, sitting up straighter and placing the rose out of sight on her lap. "Thanks, Alice."

"Sure thing, honey." Alice took elaborate care setting up Tanner's napkin and fork. She put down both cups of coffee and then positioned Tanner's pie squarely in front of him. "If that's not warm enough, or if the ice cream's too melted, just send it back and I'll fix you another one," she said.

"I'm sure it'll be fine."

Alice glanced from him to Dori. "I hope so. I truly do."

After Alice left, Tanner made no move to pick up his fork.

"Start eating," Dori suggested, "before the pie gets cold or the ice cream turns into soup. You can't put off enjoying pie à la mode."

He pushed the plate aside and concentrated the power of those incredible blue eyes on her. "I'm learning that life's like that, too. Which is as good an explanation as any for why I'm not leaving."

Her heartbeat quickened. "Look, I didn't realize how nasty Jimmy Jr. would get if somebody actually showed an interest in me. I guess I was hoping he was mostly hot air."

"Maybe he is. I think we should find out."

She shook her head. "No. Go back to Dallas and pick out somebody else from your bushel basket of letters. I know there must be a lot, with someone who looks like you."

The corner of his mouth tilted upward, which made him even more appealing. "I'll take that as a compliment."

Heat climbed into her cheeks again, but she braved it out. "I guess it was."

"And encouragement. Apparently, you find me reasonably acceptable so far."

That was the understatement of the year, Dori thought. From the way he filled out the shoulders of his Western shirt, she could imagine how he looked without it. The image was enough to make her faint with desire. "I . . . think you're very attractive." She made a grab for her coffee to hide her nervousness and promptly scalded her tongue.

"And I think you're the most beautiful woman I've seen in a long time." His quiet declaration brought her startled gaze back to his face. "You don't even know how beautiful you are, do you?"

"You're embarrassing me, Tanner."

"Why? You should be used to having people tell you you're beautiful. These truckers should mention it about every five minutes, if they have eyes in their heads."

"Well, they don't mention it. So there."

He regarded her thoughtfully. "They might be afraid Devaney would find out and have a fit. How about him? Did he ever compliment you on your looks?"

"He used to say I was 'passably pretty.'"

Tanner grimaced. "What a guy."

"Well, that's a fair description of me, after all. I wasn't even elected homecoming queen, just one of the attendants."

"You married Devaney right out of high school, didn't you?"

Dori nodded. "My folks tried to talk me out of it, but at eighteen I thought I knew everything. Jimmy Jr. was the catch of the town, three years older than me and the only son of James Devaney who owned the biggest business in Los Lobos. I had you drive past there on the way in."

"I wondered if that was on purpose."

"It was. I wanted you to see how important that name was in Los Lobos, because I thought it would help explain everything, when the time came."

Tanner leaned back against the booth. "I think I get the picture. Devaney snapped you up when you were still naive enough to believe he was a prince and you, being 'passably pretty,' were lucky to snag him. He probably thought he'd undermine your confidence enough to keep you shackled to him."

Dori had considered the very same thing, but hearing Tanner say it gave her self-confidence a big boost.

"But the thing he knew then," Tanner continued, "and what he understands even more now, is that you were the catch, Dori. If he had nothing else going for him, he had vision. He could imagine how you'd grow more beautiful every day. Only he didn't count on your spirit being stronger than his."

She drank in his words as if she were dying of thirst. "It's been so hard, Tanner. Especially after he took Little Jim away."

Tanner leaned forward. "And when am I going to meet your son?"

With a great effort, she brought herself back to reality. Not looking at him made the next statement easier. "You're not. I want you to head back tomorrow and forget all about me."

He regarded her quietly. "No can do."

She kept her face averted as she swallowed the lump that rose in her throat. "Of course you can. Just get up right now and walk out of here. Be smart, Tanner. Do it."

He cupped her chin and guided her face around until she was forced to look into his eyes. "I hate the idea of dealing with a jerk like Devaney, and I'd rather not have to. But when I walked into the Double Nickel tonight and saw you, I felt as if I'd won the lottery. I can't allow Jimmy Devaney, Jr., to spoil my chances with you."

She stared at him, her senses reeling from his touch and the magnetism of his gaze. *I felt as if I'd won the lottery,* he'd said. "What time is it?" she murmured.

Looking perplexed, he nevertheless released her chin to glance at his bare wrist. An untanned strip of skin revealed where he normally wore a watch, but for some reason it was gone. He frowned and looked up at the clock on the wall behind her. "Almost ten. Why?"

"No. Tell me exactly."

"Nine fifty-nine."

She smiled at him. "I thought so."

"I suppose that's significant because it has two nines in it?"

"It's a really lucky number for me, Tanner." A Mac Davis song provided a backdrop to the murmur of voices in the café as she gazed at him and dared to hope that he represented a change in her fortunes.

"A lucky number for me, too, I guess. From the look on your face, you've decided to let me stay."

She took a deep breath. "Yes."

"Then how about a little walk in the moonlight, Ms. Fitzpatrick?"

"I'd love it."

He reached for his billfold, pulled out some money and tucked it under his saucer. "Let's go." He held out his hand to her.

Dori picked up her rose and scooted across the seat toward him. Before she took his hand, she glanced at the denomination on the folded bill he'd left for Alice, and she gasped. "Tanner, that's way too much."

"I don't care. It was worth every penny. Come on."

Dori snatched up the money and shoved it at him. "Take this back. I'll settle with Alice on Tuesday."

"No. I—"

"Tanner, are you trying to dazzle me by throwing money around? Because that doesn't impress me one bit. I told you that in my letters."

Tanner looked away and rubbed a hand over his face. When he turned back, he smiled and took the money she held out, but she could tell it wasn't an easy thing for him to do. "Thanks, Dori. Thanks a lot."

"Sure thing." As she left the booth and walked out of the café with her hand in his, Dori vowed to watch Tanner's spending habits carefully. She appreciated generous tippers as much as any waitress, but not if a person couldn't afford the extra. Tanner might be gorgeous, courageous and kind, but if he couldn't handle money she wanted to know it before she or her heart made any promises.

3

TANNER SCANNED THE AREA looking for any sign of Devaney when he and Dori walked out into the café parking lot. The air was surprisingly warm for the middle of October, and Dori's ex-husband was nowhere in sight.

Dori glanced up into the sky. "There is a moon tonight," she said. "I was hoping it could be full, but instead it looks sort of—"

"Like a guy with a beer belly," Tanner finished for her.

Dori laughed and he wondered how many jokes he could come up with so he could make her do that again. Her laughter contained a ripple of sensuality that suggested moments to come, experiences they didn't know each other well enough yet to share. A diesel pulled away from the gas pumps and its air brakes wheezed before it rumbled down the road toward the interstate. The fumes didn't add much to the ambience, and Dori's highly visible white uniform was making Tanner uneasy. He wasn't going to back away from a fight, but he'd rather not be ambushed now, before...before what? Before he'd even had a chance to kiss her? Maybe.

She glanced up at him shyly. "I'm out of practice with this sort of thing, but I remember when I was in high school, Jimmy Jr. and I used to drive out one of the back roads to be alone."

He gave her a quick look.

"Not that I'm suggesting we rush into anything physical," she added quickly. "In fact, I think that's a big mistake couples often make."

"Probably," he agreed with some reluctance.

"But we could take that moonlit walk you mentioned, and get to know each other."

"Are you sure you trust me enough to go out to a deserted back road with me?"

Her expression was adorably serious. "Nowadays that could work both ways. Maybe I'm planning to plunge a knife into your heart and steal you blind. Women do that sort of thing, too."

He realized that. Figuratively speaking, he'd suspected those were the motives of the past couple of women he'd dated, which was why he was here with Dori, who professed not to care about material wealth. That reminded him of his role as a hand-to-mouth construction worker. "But that would be a waste of time, trying to steal from somebody like me," he said. "You're the one who should be careful, considering you have the more valuable assets."

Dori gave him a wry smile. "I'm certainly not a virgin anymore, Tanner."

"I didn't expect you to be. Little Jim had to come from somewhere, didn't he?" He looked around the parking lot. "Where's your car? You can show me this lonely road where we can be alone."

She ushered him over to a somewhat battered white Pontiac Sunbird convertible. "I think it's warm enough to put the top down," she said once they'd climbed into the car and she'd laid the rose across the dashboard. They each unlatched their side and she lowered the canvas top.

Then she reached across his knees, brushing them just enough to make him a little crazy, and opened the glove compartment.

The city women he'd known had always been concerned about their hair becoming disarranged, so her preparations for driving with the top down intrigued him. She took out an elasticized piece of fabric from the glove compartment and wound it around her hair at the nape of her neck. He would have loved to do it for her, but watching her efficient movements as she worked with the silky strands was almost as inspirational. Before this evening ended he hoped he'd be allowed to run his fingers through her glorious hair. Surely that wouldn't be pushing her self-imposed limits. After all, the whole purpose of *Texas Men* was to bring couples together, and not just for conversation.

She backed the car out of the parking space and headed toward town, but before she reached the main drag she swung left onto a two-lane road. A small subdivision on the right gave way to cotton fields anchored with square little structures, some with lights glowing from the windows.

He turned his head to watch strands of her hair work loose from their tie and whip around her cheeks. "Where do you live?" he asked.

"On the other side of town. I found a small house for rent not far from the Devaneys'. Little Jim's bedroom window is on the second floor, and I can see his light from my backyard."

Tanner's heart wrenched, imagining Dori standing in her yard staring at that shining square of light that represented her son's presence. "It sounds as if you came out of that divorce with nothing. How did that happen?"

"My own stupid fault. I was so sick of Jimmy Jr.'s using his money to get what he wanted that I asked for the minimum child support and no alimony. Jimmy Jr. thought I'd come running back after a few months of poverty. When I didn't, he got tired of waiting and sued for custody of Little Jim on the grounds that he could give him a better home. He won. That's it."

Partway through the explanation Tanner began regretting that Devaney hadn't instigated a fight in the parking lot. Tanner would have loved an opportunity to punch the guy right now.

"When I wrote to you, I didn't put all my cards on the table," Dori said.

Neither did I. Tanner's conscience pricked him. "For example?"

"What I said is true, as far as it goes. I am looking for male companionship."

Her statement sounded so formal, he couldn't resist teasing her. "You could get a little boy dog."

She blew out an exasperated sigh. "You know what I mean."

"Not really." He gave her an amused glance. "You have all those truckers to talk to nearly every day."

"All right! I miss being held, being kissed and . . . all that. Is that plain enough for you?"

"It's music to my ears, Dori." *And damn stimulating to the rest of me, too.*

"But don't you get the idea that I'm easy!"

"I would never get that idea."

"I mean it! Because my real reason for wanting to get married again has nothing to do with sex."

"That's too bad."

"I'm being perfectly honest with you, Tanner. Stop making fun of me."

"Sorry." But he was having trouble controlling his thoughts as they skimmed down the moonlit road and the houses became few and far between. The air streaming past his cheeks was cool, but not cold. It was a perfect night for lovers, and here was Dori talking about kissing and . . . all that.

"I've been getting advice from friends, and they think if I remarry and establish a two-parent household, I'll stand a better chance of getting Little Jim back. That's the real reason I wrote to you, Tanner. So if that makes you mad, I'll turn this car around and head straight for the Double Nickel."

Tanner knew he couldn't sound as disappointed as he felt or Dori really would cancel the whole thing. Her son was obviously the most important person in the world to her, and he couldn't blame her for wanting him back. Her solution was logical and practical, even if it took the romance right out of the situation they were in. He was simply the means to an end.

Hell, if she wanted a husband in a hurry, he could propose now and in no time enjoy those conjugal rights he'd been dreaming about ever since he first saw her. No time for courtship or falling in love, but a whale of a good time in bed, no doubt. Dori wouldn't welch on that part of the bargain, and she might even enjoy it.

He spoke carefully. "If all you really want is a husband, then why don't we fly up to Vegas and get married tonight? By tomorrow you can begin filing those papers to get custody of your little boy."

Her screeching stop and abrupt U-turn caught him by surprise and he whacked his shoulder against the car door. "Hey! Take it easy!"

"I won't," she said through clenched teeth. "And you can go straight to Dallas and be damned!" She peeled out in a spurt of gravel that sent the rose tumbling into his lap.

He was thrown back against the seat as she bore down on the gas. "What? What did I say? I was only trying to give you what you wanted!" He wondered if she always drove like a maniac.

"That is *not* what I want."

He glanced at the speedometer and decided it would help his peace of mind if he didn't look at it again as the wind created by her speed buffeted them. "But you said—"

"My goal is to provide a two-parent household for Little Jim. But I intend to do it *right*. What you have in mind is like throwing up a house with warped wood and rusty nails, hoping the whole thing will hold together after you slap some stucco over the crooked parts! My daddy's in construction, too, and he taught me that nothing's worth building unless it's built to last!"

Tanner forgot about the perils of taking a Texas farm road at ninety miles an hour as her statement hit him like a bowling ball aimed at his chest. He'd been waiting a lifetime to hear a woman say that. "Turn the car around."

"Not until you take back what you said."

"I take it back! I didn't like the idea, either, but I felt so sorry for you, wanting custody of your little boy, that I—"

"Sorry for me?" she cried, and stepped down harder on the gas. "That's worse!"

"Okay, not sorry! Forget sorry! Sympathetic! God, Dori, I want to help! Stop this damned car so we won't be killed before I can explain!"

Fortunately, the road was deserted, because Dori burned rubber as she slammed on the brakes, throwing them both hard against the seat belts. She turned her head in his direction. Her dark eyes blazed and her jaw was set. "Okay, start explaining."

He took a steadying breath. "You drive fast."

"Only when I'm mad. And never when Little Jim's in the car. Now talk, and you'd better not make any more immoral suggestions, or so help me, I'm taking you straight back to the Double Nickel."

Unsnapping his seat belt was a calculated risk. If this didn't work and only increased her anger, he'd be socked around like a punching bag when she peeled out again. He took off his hat and set it, along with her rose, on the dashboard before facing her. "I'm sorry I suggested getting married before we could learn to know each other, learn to love each other." He closed the gap between them slowly, as if she were a wild animal whose confidence he must win. "You're right. That would be a mortal sin."

She watched him warily but with complete absorption. He touched her cheek, and she didn't flinch. Good.

"I won't insult you like that again, Dori." Her cheek was softer than the petals of the rose he'd brought her.

Desire burned slow and steady in his groin, but his touch was light, his tone gentle. "Please give me a chance to show you I know how to build without rushing."

Her angry gaze mellowed and her lips parted ever so slightly.

He smoothed a strand of hair back behind her ear. "If you'll let me, I'll put up a solid foundation, and only use the truest wood and the strongest nails." He drew closer, and sweet heaven, she didn't move away. "This is the most important task I'll ever have in this world," he murmured as her wildflower scent threatened his control. "Trust me, and I'll do everything in my power to get it right."

Then he kissed her, slowly and with a restraint that nearly killed him. Velvet and honey beckoned him to deepen the kiss. He almost gave in and took her fully. But a shred of sanity remained, and he lifted his head to gaze into dark eyes that spoke of surrender. He wanted to shout with joy, but he swallowed his triumph and reminded himself that he'd only mortared the first brick in place. Heart pounding, he settled back in his seat and buckled his seat belt. Then he replaced his hat and tugged on the brim, as if for emphasis.

She sat looking at him for a full minute. Then, with a small smile, she swung the convertible in a lazy turn and headed away from civilization once more. He closed his eyes in gratitude. Maybe this argument would be the rockiest part of their relationship, he thought. Then he remembered Devaney. But after that kiss he'd vastly increased his estimate of what he'd tolerate just to be near Dori Fitzpatrick.

DORI GRIPPED THE WHEEL tight to keep from trembling. No man had ever talked to her like that, echoing her belief in the sanctity of marriage, a belief she carried like a precious jewel deep in her soul despite her disillusionment with Jimmy. A first kiss had never felt like that, either—so rich, yet so brief. She wanted more, although after all her speeches she couldn't let Tanner know that. At least not yet.

Maybe everything had to do with her lucky number. She'd never put it to such a critical test, but Tanner seemed to be the one she'd been destined for all her life. Still, before she became too dizzy to think clearly, she'd better find out more about this apparent dream man.

"I've—" She paused and cleared her throat. Talking wasn't so easy after a kiss like Tanner's. "I've explained why I wrote in to the magazine," she said. "But I've wondered ever since I saw your picture why in the world you were in it."

He hesitated a few seconds before answering. "I guess the simple truth is I was lonely."

"Lonely? Was there a plague that killed off all the women in Dallas?"

He chuckled.

"Come on, Tanner. I may be a small-town girl, but I'm not stupid. If you were lonely, all you'd have had to do was stroll into one of those singles' bars I've heard about and find yourself somebody. I guarantee women would be hanging all over you, with a body like yours." Dori realized what she'd said and winced. So much for playing it cool. "What I meant to say is—"

"Don't change a thing, Dori." He was laughing now. "I liked the statement the way it was."

"Don't be getting a big head, Mr. Jones. Handsome is as handsome does. So, did you have dates or not?"

"I had dates," he admitted.

"Ha. I knew it. You'll have to come up with a better reason than loneliness for putting your picture in that magazine."

"Nope. That's it. I had dates, but they always seemed to be with the wrong kind of women for me. I couldn't imagine taking any of them home to my mom and dad and introducing them as my wife."

My wife. The phrase, coming from Tanner, sounded warm and intimate, the exact opposite of the belligerent, possessive way Jimmy had always said it. "That's important to you, what your folks think of your wife?"

"Yep, sure is."

"And what wouldn't your parents have liked about these women you've been dating?"

"They seemed to be focused on material things."

Dori smiled, relieved to have something make sense at last. "Well, I can tell you why. Flashing twenty-dollar bills around the way you did in the café is a surefire way to attract women who like spending money." She sent him a look of triumph.

"You may have a point."

"Of course I do. Now, I don't think much of a stingy man, either, but you can't give a woman the impression you plan to buy her any little thing her heart desires. Greedy women will be on you like flies on horse poop."

"What if I told you I want to buy you any little thing your heart desires?"

She turned down a dirt road and slowed so as not to stir up too much dust. "In the first place, I wouldn't believe a word of it. Unless you planned to run up a huge debt. Don't forget, I've lived around construction workers all my life. My daddy and momma had to leave Los Lobos and move to San Antonio because that's where the work was. Just about killed them to leave me and Little Jim, especially when I had to go through all that trouble. They tried to loan me money to hire a good lawyer, but I couldn't take it. They don't have any to spare. I'm sure you don't, either. Throwing money around makes me think a man is either stupid or trying to make up for some sort of sexual inadequacy."

Tanner seemed to be caught in a coughing fit.

Concerned, Dori pulled to the shoulder of the road and shut off the ignition. "What's wrong? Are you allergic to dust or something?"

"No," he choked out.

She realized he was laughing. That had been the cause of his coughing fit. "What's so funny now?"

"Which—" He gasped and shook his head. "Which do you think I am?"

"Which what?"

"Stupid or sexually inadequate?"

"Oh." She remembered his potent kiss and doubted he was lacking in that area. Neither did he seem particularly stupid. "Well, I'll make an allowance for this being an unusual situation. But if you kept doing that, I'd be worried."

"With luck I'd get the stupid label."

Her body warmed at his implication that soon she'd have discovered he wasn't inadequate. "People in our circumstances have to be careful with money, Tanner. I don't put a great deal of importance on it, but on the other hand, we need a certain amount to live on, and there's always our old age to be considered."

He was quiet for a moment. "I got the strangest tingle down my spine when you said *our old age.*" He turned to her. "What do you think, Dori? Is there a chance we'll grow old together? Can you picture rocking chairs on the porch and visits from the grandkids?"

Her heart thudded in her chest. "I don't know."

He opened his door and unlatched his seat belt. "Come on. Let's take that walk in the moonlight."

When she joined him at the front of the car he slipped his fingers through hers and they started down the dirt road as if they'd been taking walks together for years. Water ran in an irrigation ditch nearby, filling the air with the scent of rain. Dori tried to remember a single time she'd ever taken a walk with Jimmy Jr. They'd driven out to the back roads when they were dating, of course. But Jimmy hadn't wanted to leave the car, or more specifically, the back seat.

Dori paused and lifted her chin skyward. "Look up," she said. "And take off your hat."

He lifted off his hat by the crown and held it against his thigh as he gazed into the night sky. "My God. I've never seen so many stars. They go all the way to the horizon."

"Because there's nothing to block them. No mountains, almost no trees. You should see a sunset out here, Tanner. The whole sky's on fire."

He stood quietly for a while. "It's not just Little Jim holding you in Los Lobos, is it?"

"No. I was raised here, and I got used to having all that empty space around me. When I go where there are lots of trees, or mountains cutting out the view, I get claustrophobia." She also suspected why he'd asked the question. His home was East Texas. "There's talk of construction work picking up in the area," she said. "My daddy's keeping track of it, because he and Momma would love to move back."

When he didn't respond right away, she glanced at him. He was staring off into the distance, seemingly lost in thought.

"I know it seems stark at first, but give yourself a chance to get used to the openness," she said. "How long have you lived in East Texas?"

He brought his attention back to her. "About fifteen years." He squeezed her hand and replaced his hat as they started down the road again. Crickets chirped in the dry grass beside the road. "It's not the terrain that I'm in love with, although some of it's real pretty, Dori. I'd like you to see it. Lakes so blue you'd swear somebody dropped food coloring in them. But the . . . business opportunities are better there."

"You need to talk to my daddy. What's your trade?"

"I've done a little of everything. I have both a carpenter's and an electrician's license. I can frame when necessary and drywall in a pinch."

"Goodness, Tanner. You could find a job around here, I'll bet." She paused, becoming unsure of herself. "If you wanted to," she said more softly. "We shouldn't get ahead of ourselves, should we? I mean, you haven't even met Little Jim yet."

"Tomorrow, right?"

"It's my day with him. He wants to go see the Power Rangers movie again, and it's finally come back to the budget movie house in Abilene. That may not seem too exciting, but—"

"Dori, you have something to learn." He pulled her to a stop and caught her other hand to bring her around in front of him. "Just being with you at last is exciting to me. And I think something low-key like going to the movies is a perfect way to start out with Little Jim. Besides, I don't know who the Power Rangers are. Sounds as if I'd better learn if I expect to have anything in common with him."

"That's for sure." She smiled with relief that he approved of her plans. "I thought that would be a low-cost thing we could all do together, and he loves McDonald's, so we don't have to spend a lot of money entertaining him. He's not used to that from me, anyway. Just from Jimmy Jr."

"I think I can manage a budget movie house and McDonald's," Tanner said with a trace of sarcasm. "Maybe I can even squeeze out enough for an ice-cream cone on the way home."

"Now, don't take that tone! Remember what I said about throwing money around."

He chuckled. "I doubt I'll ever forget. Every time I reach for my wallet I'll wonder if I'm displaying my sexual inadequacies."

She gazed at him standing before her in the moonlight, his face cast in shadow from the brim of his hat. In his yoked Western shirt and snug-fitting jeans he projected the epitome of all her sexual fantasies. Her pulse quickened and she couldn't look away.

"You'd better stop that," he said.

"Stop what?" she murmured.

"Looking at me like that."

"Why?"

"Because it makes me want to kiss the living daylights out of you."

The blood sang in her ears. "Maybe that's exactly what I want you to do."

4

TANNER HADN'T HEARD such a tempting invitation in a long while. The first kiss had been an experiment and could have become a disaster, but this time Dori had asked.

She stood before him, her uniform carving an alabaster silhouette against the night sky. Stars twinkled around her shoulders and tangled in the windblown tresses of her hair. Her gaze lifted to his with the innocence of a child, but the seductive curve of her mouth suggested the passion of a woman. Tanner was too entranced to move.

She smiled and guided his hands around her waist. "You're not going to turn shy on me now, are you?"

"Not shy, just dazzled." His fingers encountered the warm cotton of her uniform. He discovered he could span her waist with his hands as he drew her close and savored the first soft contact with her breasts.

"My goodness." Her breathing became shallow as she gazed up at him. "I don't recall ever dazzling a man before."

"I'm sure you have." His glance traveled over her face, memorizing the graceful arch of her eyebrows, the fathomless depths of her eyes, the beckoning fullness of her mouth. "You just didn't know it."

"You'd better not be overcome by it." She reached for his hat and dangled it from the brim behind his back as she wound her arms around his neck. "You haven't kissed me yet."

Her taunt almost destroyed his control, but he took a deep breath and maintained his equilibrium. She might be used to a grab-and-grope kind of guy, but he wanted to separate himself from that type of low-life lover. Smiling, he slid his fingers through her luxuriant hair and found the elastic fabric holding it captive. "When I was a kid I was always the slowest at eating an ice-cream cone, too. I figured when something was that good, you should make it last." He eased the circle of material from her hair and tucked it into his back pocket. "And this," he continued, burying his fingers in her hair once again, "is going to be very good."

"Oh." The word came out almost as a sigh.

"And very slow." He lightly massaged her scalp and combed his hands through her hair, reveling in the silken richness that slid through his fingers.

Her eyes drifted closed in pleasure.

"You are a rare and beautiful woman, Dori."

Her eyelids fluttered open and she gazed at him.

"One who deserves to be treated with tenderness and care." He bunched her hair in his fist and inhaled its sweet aroma before releasing it, letting it tumble down the slope of her breast. "One who deserves a lover who takes his time."

"You're a sweet-talkin' man, Tanner," she said. "I've been warned about men like you."

"Have you?" He cupped her cameo-perfect face in both hands and brushed his thumbs across her elegant cheekbones. Every touch bought a jolt of pleasure that settled deep within him and fed the fire. "And what have you been warned about?"

"Momma always said a sweet-talkin' man could break your heart."

"So can an ugly-talking one," he said gently.

A flash of sorrow in her eyes made his heart ache. "True," she whispered.

"I don't intend to break your heart." He dropped a light kiss on her brow, and when she closed her eyes once more in surrender, he moved his lips to each quivering eyelid. "I intend to make it sing."

She took a long, shuddering breath as he feathered kisses at her temple, her earlobe, the curve of her jaw. As he dipped to the hollow of her throat, he savored the creamy texture of skin that heated beneath his lazy ministrations. When his lips returned to her cheek and found the corner of her mouth, she moaned softly. He moved with deliberate care to the other corner. She murmured his name.

"I'm here." He hovered close and drank in the warmth of her breath on his face. "Right here." When at last he brought his mouth down to hers, the pleasure was so intense he felt as if he might explode in her arms.

He abandoned himself to the ripe bounty, growing dizzy on the riches she offered. He'd had no idea, he thought fleetingly. No idea at all. He felt himself drowning in her eagerness as she parted her lips and invited him inside. He shifted the angle of his mouth to go deeper and she welcomed him with a little whimper that roused him to a frenzy of wanting—wanting that made him crush her closer and increase the pressure on those sweet lips. Wanting that had to be overruled. Somehow.

With a groan he wrenched his mouth from hers. Chest heaving, he relaxed his grip and stepped back, but the look in her eyes still held him prisoner.

She struggled with her breathing, too. "I...think you...did," she managed to whisper.

He fought for air and cleared his throat. "Did what?"

"Kissed...the living daylights out of me."

Laughter helped, but he was still trembling with need. "Unfortunately, that's not all I want to do right now."

Her gaze drifted downward to the aching bulge in his jeans. "That's not unfortunate," she murmured. "Just premature."

"Would you think I'm crude if I asked by how much?"

Her dark eyes sparkled. "Are you asking for a construction timetable?"

"Yes...no. No." He pushed aside the urge to haul her against him for another round. "But if we're going to postpone making love to each other, you'll have to help me out."

"I will, Tanner." Her smile was mysterious and knowing. "If you hadn't stopped just now, I would have stopped you."

"If you say so," he said cautiously, not quite sure he believed it. She was still too close for comfort, and he started to back away from the temptation she presented.

She grabbed his arm. "Careful where you step. I dropped your hat while you were kissing me."

"Did you now?" He gave her a long look.

"Well, yes. I got a little carried away, but I still could have stopped you. I was in command of myself enough for that."

"I see."

"Don't be difficult. Certainly you agree that we need to get acquainted on many levels before we satisfy ourselves sexually?"

"Of course," he said. The concept of satisfying themselves, especially with the delightful drawl she gave the word *satisfy,* sounded pretty darned appealing at the moment.

Her eyebrows lifted as if she expected a more complete answer.

"I'm sure it's a very good idea to become friends before we become lovers." He tried to say it with conviction.

"I've read a lot on the subject," she said. "You see, if we're friends first, and the lovemaking isn't perfect, we'll be able to work through that."

He couldn't help laughing. "After that kiss, you doubt whether we'll be good together? Get real, Dori. Physically, we're a perfect match. You know it and I know it."

A pulse beat in her throat, and she swallowed before replying. "Okay, let's say we are physically compatible, and we make love tonight."

His heart thudded in his chest. He'd give several years of his life for that chance.

Her voice quivered just a little, betraying her banked passion, but she soldiered on with a determination he found endearing. "If we made love tonight," she said, "we could be blinded by sexual excitement and miss the signs that we weren't compatible otherwise."

He grinned and stuck out his hand. "Meet Tanner Jones, who's already a blind man."

She batted his hand away. "That's ridiculous. One little kiss. Surely you can still be objective about our relationship."

"Speak for yourself."

She sighed mightily. "Then apparently I have to do the job for both of us. Momma always said men think with their . . . male equipment."

Tanner chuckled and turned around to retrieve his hat. As he dusted it off, he glanced at her. "And what were you thinking with when you dropped my hat in the dirt?"

"I . . . I was—"

"Dori, we're no different. Both of us are crazy to make love, but if you want to wait, we'll wait. It won't be easy, but I guess when we finally do give in, the whole experience will be better." He paused and gazed at her. "If that's even remotely possible."

Dori clasped her hands in front of her and gave him a long, approving glance.

He pointed a finger at her. "And stop that. I'm only human, and that look is what got us started in the first place."

"I'm just so pleased with you, Tanner. That's all."

"Pleased with me?" He didn't think any woman had said those words to him before. He kind of liked it, but he wasn't sure he understood what she meant. "Why?"

"For respecting my wishes."

He thought about that while he adjusted his hat. It didn't take much imagination to picture Devaney riding roughshod over any idea she had, so he guessed it would be a big deal to her if a man paid attention to what she said. He shrugged. "I've gone out with women who didn't really mean it when they told me no. Unfortunately for them, I always stop when a woman asks me to. I don't enjoy playing those guessing games."

"I don't play games."

"I'm counting on that." He longed to touch her again but didn't dare. He braced his hands on his hips to keep himself from reaching for her. "Better take me back, Dori."

"Right." She started down the road, and he fell into step beside her. "You did make reservations at the Prairie Schooner Motel and RV Park, like I suggested?"

"I did." And secretly he'd hoped he could cancel that reservation, but it didn't look as if Dori would invite him home with her tonight. His more noble self argued that she was absolutely right in delaying their lovemaking. But his baser self was frustrated as hell.

AFTER LEAVING TANNER at the Double Nickel, Dori drove home to her two-bedroom tract home. Although most of her neighbors were low-income families struggling to get by, they kept up their yards and applied paint to the wooden trim of the stucco homes when necessary. Cardboard pumpkins and witches were taped to many front windows in anticipation of Halloween two weeks away. It was the sort of street she could feel safe taking little Jim trick-or-treating on—if she'd be allowed to do that this year. Halloween fell on a Thursday, which wasn't her day. Her jaw clenched at the reminder of all Jimmy Jr. had stolen from her.

She wasn't surprised to see Jimmy's big truck backed up into her driveway, blocking her way into her garage. She half expected him to turn on the spotlights mounted on the cab roof in an effort to frighten her into a dazed panic the way he trapped deer when he went hunting at night.

She pulled up at the curb so he'd have a way out when he left. And he was definitely leaving.

As she got out of the car he materialized from the shadows and sauntered toward her. "Where you been, Dori Mae? It's after eleven, and accordin' to Travis Neff, you left the Double Nickel at nine-thirty."

"You should be ashamed of yourself, making Travis spy on me like that."

"It just came up in conversation when I dropped in there about ten. After all, you and that ol' boy from Dallas were making quite a spectacle of yourselves. Can't expect people not to talk."

"Go home, Jimmy." She could smell beer on his breath, but he wasn't drunk. His speech was too precise, his gaze too clear, for him to be impaired by alcohol. She started past him.

He stepped in front of her again. "What do you think you're doin', bringing that ol' boy to town? Trying to make me jealous, Dori Mae?"

"No." She hated the thought that he'd create a scene in her front yard. Some of the neighbors had been a little suspicious of her moving in. Not only was she the only divorcée on the block, she'd defied the powerful Devaneys to gain that status, which labeled her a troublemaker. But in the two years she'd lived in the neighborhood, she'd proven to everyone that she could live as respectable a life as the traditional families surrounding her. Screaming fights on the front lawn weren't part of that picture.

"Then maybe you're getting a little lonely. Is that it, darlin'?"

She had an uneasy feeling where this was headed.

"Because if you want a little action, you know right where to come," he drawled. "We had us some good times in bed, sugar."

She remembered that he'd had some good times. At first she'd been happy to make him feel good and figured eventually he'd want the same thing for her. Then she'd begun to realize that he was as selfish in lovemaking as he was in everything else. "That's over with, Jimmy."

"I'll be damned if it is." He made a grab for her, but she pushed him away. "Don't be like that, sweetheart," he whined, but he stayed put. A few months after the divorce he'd tried to force himself on her and she'd kneed him in the crotch. A friend had suggested she might require some self-defense to handle Jimmy, and she'd practiced with a dummy she'd made from an old pair of jeans stuffed with rags. Jimmy hadn't tried anything similar since.

"Look, I'm only trying to get on with my life," she said. "And I wish you'd do the same."

"But that's the problem. You belong in my life, but you're too danged stubborn to see it. Little Jim misses you something fierce."

Dori's heart twisted at the mention of her son. "Then let him live with me," she said, although she knew she was wasting her breath.

"Here?" Jimmy swept an arm back toward her little house. "Is that how you want him to grow up? You don't even have a computer, Dori Mae. In fact, you don't have a damn thing to offer that boy."

Except all my love. But she didn't say it. "Let me by, Jimmy. It's late, and we both have things to do tomorrow."

"Don't think I don't remember tomorrow's Monday. That ol' boy from Dallas better be gone tomorrow. I don't want him within ten miles of Little Jim. You got that?"

"Good night, Jimmy." She shoved past him and started toward her front door, opening her purse on the way. She kept pepper spray on her key chain.

He didn't follow her, but he didn't leave, either. "You could lose those Mondays, you know," he said, raising his voice. "If the judge was to hear that you'd been behaving like a common streetwalker in front of the boy, he'd probably want to take those Monday visitations away."

She winced at how that would sound to any neighbors with their windows open on this warm night. She put the key in the lock with trembling fingers. Jimmy's threat was ridiculous, of course. But she'd thought his threat about getting custody of Little Jim had been ridiculous, too.

"It's just your pride making you act this way, Dori Mae. You can't admit you made a mistake walkin' out on me. That's okay. I won't ask you to apologize, like some guys might. Just come back, and everything will be fine."

Dori was afraid any response would only escalate the conflict. She opened the door.

"You'll come back," Jimmy called out as she stepped inside. "I guarantee you'll come back!"

Dori closed the door and latched the dead bolt. Shaking, she leaned against the doorjamb. She'd never hated anyone in her life until Jimmy took away her son. But she'd never loved anyone as much as she did Little Jim. If Tanner Jones wouldn't marry her and give her a chance to get Little Jim back, then she'd do whatever she had to do in order to be with her son every day. Even if that meant crawling on her hands and knees back to Jimmy Devaney, Jr.

DORI WOKE BEFORE the alarm buzzed, as she did every Monday morning these days. And as she did every morning, especially on Mondays, she said hello to Little Jim. Unfortunately, it was a picture of him and not the real thing that grinned back at her when she wished him a good morning. The picture was her current favorite and sat in a small frame on her bedside table. In the snapshot he stood in her backyard, his right arm cocked as if to throw the football she'd given him for his last birthday.

But he was only pretending, because he would never have risked throwing the ball at her and perhaps hurting her or breaking the camera. The camera was their lifeline. Every Monday she took a roll of Little Jim for herself. Then she let him take a roll of her so he'd have a whole new batch of pictures every week. She didn't know what he did with his pictures of her, but she'd covered the walls of her bedroom with snapshots of her son. For now, it was all she could think to do.

She threw back the covers and got out of bed as nervous excitement churned in her stomach. She glanced out the bedroom window at a sky that reminded her of a blue pillow slept on by a white cat. The wispy clouds didn't look as if they held rain. She was glad of that. Plenty of things could go wrong today, and it was nice to know the weather wouldn't be one of them.

She lived neatly, but her little house was cleaner than usual this morning. If all went well, Tanner would visit her here before the week was over. Therefore, she'd rearranged her sparse secondhand furniture and vacuumed the corners of every room. She'd washed the bright curtains she'd sewn for the windows and set out vases of yellow and white chrysanthemums from her yard. Padding barefoot from room to room, she studied the effect. Tanner would like it, she decided. He'd stated clearly in his letters that he didn't care for pretension. With her income and legal debts, she didn't have to worry about offending him on that score.

She dressed in jeans and a Power Rangers T-shirt that matched the one Little Jim would no doubt wear today. She'd found the T-shirts on sale and they'd become a Monday uniform for mother and son, a subtle show of solidarity. Then she plaited her hair into a long braid down her back in anticipation that Little Jim would want to ride to Abilene with the convertible top down.

Standing at the sink with one eye on the clock, she forced herself to eat a piece of toast and drink a glass of orange juice. She didn't want to be starving by the time lunch came, considering that Tanner would probably insist on picking up the tab. Judging from his clothes and his truck, he didn't have a lot of money to spare.

Finally, she grabbed her sunglasses and her purse and headed out the door. Even after months of doing it, she hadn't become used to driving to the Devaney mansion to pick up her son. She felt more like a hired nanny than a mother as she spoke into the intercom at the iron gate and drove down the winding road toward the house. The curving entrance was pure pretension. When the Devaneys bought the property it had been flat and treeless, like most of the terrain around Los Lobos. They'd laid out the winding road up to the house and planted fast-growing cottonwoods along it, as if the trees had dictated the route and not the other way around. Dori had always figured the long route up to the house was supposed to create anticipation for what lay at the end.

In Dori's opinion, travelers up the driveway were in for a disappointment. The house squatted at the end of the road like a huge building block. No porches softened the austere lines of its two-story bulk, no bay windows added a graceful curve to the exterior and no balconies hinted at romanticism or whimsy on the part of the owners. The sole nod to architectural interest was a flurry of white shutters framing square windows cut into the redbrick facade. Dori accepted the uninspired lines of her little house because she couldn't afford better. But these people could.

She parked in the circular driveway near the front door. At least the flowers in their rectangular beds were beautiful, but then again, Dori didn't think there was such a thing as an ugly flower. If there had been, the Devaneys would have demanded the gardener plant some, she thought with a wicked smile. She gave the doorbell a firm push.

Jimmy Jr.'s mother answered the door. Dori had discovered long ago that Crystal Devaney channeled all her time and energy into keeping her job as James P. Devaney's wife. To that end she'd endured a face-lift, the rigors of a personal trainer, hunger pangs and boredom.

Then Little Jim had come into her life, and in her first and only grandchild she'd finally found a distraction that met with James P. Devaney's complete approval. In fact, the child had brought a new spark to their relationship. Dori had always known she was fighting more than Jimmy in trying to regain custody of her son. Little Jim's grandparents needed him desperately.

"Oh, hello, Dori." Crystal always sounded astonished to see Dori every Monday morning, although Dori had been appearing at precisely eight-thirty each Monday for six months. "You're welcome to come in, but I don't think Little Jim feels up to going with you today."

5

DORI FOUGHT DOWN the panic that rose within her at Crystal's statement. Not living with Little Jim when he was healthy was hard enough. Thankfully, he hadn't been sick in the time they'd been apart, but she'd dreaded the time when he'd catch some flu bug.

Cold sweat trickled down her back as she stepped inside and started for the stairs. "What's wrong with him? Does he have a fever?"

"He's not sick."

Dori turned back toward Crystal. In her casually elegant turquoise jumpsuit she could easily pass for forty instead of her true age of fifty-three. She reminded Dori of a woman posing for a hormone replacement therapy advertisement. "I thought you said he didn't feel well enough to go out today."

"I said I didn't think he'd feel up to it."

Dori tensed. "And why is that?"

"He's afraid you're taking this construction worker from Dallas along today."

A chill ran through Dori as she gazed into Crystal's eyes, the same green as Jimmy Jr.'s. "And who told him that?"

Crystal shrugged. "He could have heard it anywhere. The whole town's talking about you contacting this man through a matchmaking magazine. I kept hoping the whole thing would go away. It's quite embarrassing, really. I thought you had more class than that, Dori Mae."

"I doubt a five-year-old spends much time listening to town gossip. Someone in this house has prejudiced him against Tanner before he had a chance to form his own opinion. I suppose I should have expected that, but for some reason I didn't."

Crystal crossed her arms and stared at the Oriental hall runner beneath her feet for a moment. When she looked up again her expression had softened. "Dori, honey, I really wish you'd give Jimmy Jr. another chance. I can understand that you're lonely, but some stranger from Dallas isn't the answer. Not when you have a fine man like my Jimmy who wants to give you the world. He's just devastated about this misunderstanding you two have had. Send this construction worker home. James has offered to grant Jimmy Jr. time off so the two of you can take a second honeymoon. How does a trip to the Bahamas sound?"

Dori closed her eyes. She couldn't be upset with Crystal for offering bribes—the whole family operated that way. And of course Crystal saw nothing but good in her only son and couldn't figure out why Dori didn't want him. Dori understood that fierce mother love more than ever now that she had Little Jim. "I'm sorry, Crystal. I wish Jimmy and I were more compatible, but we're not. We never will be."

"Then at least think of the child." Crystal's voice was thick with unshed tears. "He doesn't understand why his momma and daddy don't live together anymore."

Dori gazed at her in speechless agony. There was nothing to say to that. Little Jim didn't deserve to pay the price for his parents' mistakes, but he would pay them, anyway.

"Momma?" In jeans and his Power Rangers T-shirt, Little Jim stood at the top of the stairs, not running down to her for the first time in his life.

The tears pooling in Dori's eyes blurred his image. "Hi, sweetheart."

"Daddy said some ol' boy from Dallas might come with us today, Momma," Little Jim said in a fair imitation of his father's drawl.

Dori grimaced, wondering how much else of Jimmy Jr. was rubbing off on her son. "There's a very nice man named Tanner Jones I'd like you to meet," she said. "If you really don't like him, he doesn't have to go with us."

Little Jim grabbed the banister for support and swung his leg back and forth. "Daddy says this ol' boy doesn't like kids."

"Your daddy—" Dori caught herself before she criticized Jimmy Jr. Every book she'd ever read on divorce advised against running down the ex-spouse to the child. "Your daddy might have misunderstood," she said. "Tanner likes kids a lot." Actually, Dori didn't know that for a fact, but if he didn't, he'd be history, anyway.

Crystal stepped forward. "You don't have to go today if you don't want to, L.J."

Dori hated the nickname, which made her son sound like some sort of oil baron, but she'd never told Crystal that. Little Jim didn't seem to mind, and considering all the other negative influences Dori worried about in the

Devaney household, including prejudice against women, the nickname wasn't important enough to challenge.

"If you want to stay here, we could bake those M&M cookies you like," Crystal added.

The suggestion seemed out of place coming from somebody dressed in turquoise silk, but Dori knew Crystal meant it. She'd do anything for her grandson, including tying on an apron and risking her manicure in the name of baking Little Jim's favorite cookies. Part of Dori appreciated that kind of devotion; part of her was terrified by its intensity.

Little Jim swung his leg harder, nearly upsetting his balance. "I guess I wanna see the movie," he said. "But I don't know about that ol' boy."

"Just meet him," Dori said. "If you don't want him to go after you meet him, he won't go. I promise."

"Okay."

As quickly as that, the crisis was over and Little Jim skipped down the stairs. Dori crouched down and held out her arms for their traditional hug. Little Jim squeezed her hard around the neck, and she choked back a fresh wave of tears as she breathed in his familiar boy scent that always reminded her of fresh-mown grass. She hugged him back, careful not to give in to the urge to crush him against her. She'd never allowed him to see the depth of her grief at losing him, and she never would.

"I'll go get everything ready for baking the cookies," Crystal said.

Dori glanced up at her in surprise.

"In case L.J. comes back," she added.

Dori watched her former mother-in-law walk regally back to the kitchen and felt an unexpected stab of pity.

ABOUT TEN MINUTES before nine, Tanner walked to the front parking area of the Prairie Schooner Motel and RV Park and searched for a spot to wait where he'd have an unobstructed view of the road. He chose to lean against a pole where he was shaded by a small but authentic-looking covered wagon that perched twenty-five feet over his head.

He smiled to himself. Here he was waiting for nine o'clock to roll around again and facing a whole new set of challenges. Yet he felt more prepared than he had twelve hours ago, more convinced that his plan was a good one.

He'd actually enjoyed spending the night in the clean but Spartan motel room and had opened his window to listen to crickets and the rumble of trucks on the access road. The lack of bellboys and room service was a refreshing change from his usual business trips. He'd never learned to appreciate the prestige of executive suite elevators and mints on his pillow at night. Being able to open his door and step into the fresh air appealed to him far more than a penthouse view of city lights and twenty-four-hour room service.

The motel owner, an old guy named Elmer, had seemed to know who Tanner was when he checked in, but Tanner had stopped being edgy about that. In the Dallas area he was known as the president of Jones Construction and a community leader, but here he was famous for only one thing. He was the man Dori had chosen out of *Texas Men.* After last night's kiss—the second one—he was damn grateful she had.

A sedan with three little kids in the back seat pulled up to the front office. The father got out of the car to return the room key, and the sound of bickering surged from the back seat. The mother turned and shouted to the children, and Tanner winced as the children shouted back.

He couldn't picture Dori screaming at her son that way, but he didn't know her well enough to be sure. She'd certainly reacted with fury when he'd suggested the quickie marriage in Vegas. Tanner smiled to himself. And good for her, he thought. She'd been suitably outraged by an outrageous proposal. In fact, that might have been the moment he truly began to believe in a future with Dori Fitzpatrick.

But he was still on trial. He needed to get along with Little Jim today or the whole show was over. Tanner wished he'd had more opportunity to be around little kids recently, but his younger sister was too busy becoming a trial lawyer to settle down with babies, and his social life had been spent in the company of adults for the past ten years. He felt as if he were about to take a final exam for a class he'd never attended. But he was sure of one thing—with kids, you didn't dare fake it.

To Tanner's left, a block away, the white Sunbird appeared, top down. He straightened and took a deep breath. Jimmy Jr. might turn out to be an obstacle to winning Dori, but he was a manageable one. Little Jim could make or break the relationship. Tanner didn't intend to forget that.

Dori pulled up beside him, and Tanner got his first look at her son. Tufts of copper-colored hair poked out from around his Dallas Cowboys cap, and his face and arms were sprinkled with freckles. His mouth, nose and chin reminded Tanner of Dori, but his eyes were the same shade of green as his father's. Tanner vowed not to let an accident of birth prejudice him against that green-eyed stare.

Little Jim seemed just as intent on getting his first look at Tanner. Dori remained behind the wheel instead of leaping out of the car to introduce them. She turned off the motor, pushed her sunglasses to the top of her head and gave Tanner a tentative smile. It seemed as if she didn't want to trivialize this moment with meaningless social customs.

Taking his cue from Dori, Tanner stood quietly without speaking or pasting on an ingratiating smile, and let himself be studied like a specimen under a microscope. The thoroughness of the boy's inspection indicated he understood all too well the change Tanner represented in his young life. As the son of a couple happily married for forty years, Tanner could only guess at the mental gymnastics required of this little guy.

Finally, Little Jim finished his survey and gazed straight into Tanner's eyes. "I bet you don't know who the White Ranger is," he challenged.

"You're right, I don't."

Little Jim stuck out his chest and pointed. "That's him." He glanced at Dori. "Momma's wearing him, too. We always wear these shirts on Mondays. Even if they're still in the dirty clothes hamper. We fish them out and wear them, anyway. Right, Momma?"

Tanner's amused glance flicked over to catch Dori's reaction.

She blushed at this revelation, but she supported her son's statement. "Yep. Just fish them right out and put them right on," she said.

Tanner laughed, and to his surprise, so did Little Jim. Green eyes twinkling, he covered his mouth and looked up at Tanner. Some of the tension eased in Tanner's solar plexus. Apparently, he'd just passed the first test by understanding the importance of shirts that must be worn, regardless of their condition.

Dori cleared her throat and spoke to her son. "This cowboy wanted to hitch a ride into Abilene with us. He's never seen the Power Rangers movie and he realizes that's a big gap in his education. What do you think? Should we let him go along?"

Tanner was taken aback that Dori was leaving the decision up to her son. Maybe she had her reasons for giving him that kind of power over this day they'd planned to spend together, but he suddenly realized that if Little Jim's response was thumbs-down, he'd be left standing in the parking lot. He hadn't considered that as an option.

Tanner met Little Jim's assessing glance with an outward calm that he'd perfected for dealing with belligerent subcontractors and excitable clients. But inside, his gut was churning. Usually he could figure out what adults were thinking, but a five-year-old's mind was unknown territory, unless he reached back to his own childhood for enlightenment. When he remembered what an independent little cuss he'd been at that age, he wasn't comforted.

"I guess it's okay if he comes," Little Jim said. There was no arrogance in the statement, only an underlying uneasiness.

If Tanner had anticipated dealing with a preschooler on a power trip, he needn't have worried. Little Jim wasn't interested in challenging anybody's authority. He was just plain scared. And Tanner didn't blame him, poor kid. His first five years in this world hadn't been a model of stability. Tanner began to understand Dori's single-mindedness where this tyke was concerned.

"Thank you," Tanner said to Little Jim. "I know this day with your momma is very special."

Little Jim nodded, his devotion to his mother shining in his eyes. Then he gazed up at Tanner as if he'd come to another decision. "Wanna ride in front with Momma?"

The concession, given so soon, took his breath away. "That's the most generous thing anyone's done for me in a long time," he said.

Dori chuckled as her son unbuckled his seat belt and scrambled between the bucket seats to the back. "Don't be getting a big head, Tanner. Little Jim loves riding in the back seat when the top's down. There's more wind back there. He'd do it all the time, except I refuse to look like his chauffeur, so I make him ride up front with me when it's just the two of us."

"I see." Tanner opened the passenger door and climbed in. Then he turned around and glanced at Little Jim, who was grinning at him. "You'd rather sit back there than up here with this beautiful lady?"

Little Jim's grin widened as he nodded. "Riding in the back seat is like flying."

"The funny thing is, the front seat can be like that, too." Tanner winked at Dori.

"No, it can't," Little Jim said. "The front seat is *boring*."

"Not always." Tanner caught the quick look of awareness in Dori's eyes before she pulled her sunglasses down and presented her profile to him. Pink tinged her creamy cheeks.

"Buckle up, you two," she said. "I'm starting the engine."

Tanner settled in his seat and snapped the belt over his lap before glancing over at Dori. She'd pressed her lips together in an unsuccessful attempt to hide the tiny smile creating a dimple at the corner of her mouth. Tanner hadn't felt this good in ages.

THE GOOD FEELING LASTED until sometime around four in the afternoon. Tanner was congratulating himself on how well everything had turned out as the three of them left the ice-cream shop located in an Abilene indoor shopping mall. They'd had lunch at McDonald's and sat in a nearly empty theater to see the Power Rangers movie. Dori's placement of Little Jim in the middle seat had been a wise move. The darkened theater was a tempting place with someone like Dori around, but Tanner didn't think displaying affection in front of Little Jim was a good idea yet. Just having the kid accept him as part of the excursion to Abilene was enough for now.

They'd taken endless pictures during the day, and Tanner had felt flattered to be included in a few. Now they strolled the mall in easy camaraderie while they worked off the ice-cream sundaes they'd just eaten. As they walked, Little Jim relived aloud his favorite moments from the movie.

"Momma, look!" He ran over to the window of a large toy store and stood transfixed at the display of deluxe Power Ranger figures and all their assorted gear.

Dori's small sigh of frustration was subtle, but Tanner caught it.

"Can we go in and see how much?" Little Jim asked.

"You know we can't buy any of that now," Dori said. "It doesn't matter how much it is. You'll just make yourself feel bad because you can't have it."

Little Jim turned an imploring gaze up at her. "Maybe it's on *sale.* A really big sale. Can we just see? Please, Momma?"

Tanner looked at Dori in surprise. "He doesn't have any of this stuff?"

"Not anything so fancy." She gave Tanner a look that warned him to drop the subject.

"*Please*, Momma? I don't care if I can't buy it now. I just want to look at it. Can I?"

"All right," Dori said. "You can show me one thing you want Santa to bring this year. That way I can help you spell it when you write your letter to him."

"That's easy." Little Jim marched into the store with Dori and Tanner trailing behind. "I want the White Ranger."

For Tanner, the store was a bewildering array of stuffed animals, colorful plastic toys and games he'd never heard of. He really was out of the loop when it came to this age group, he conceded silently. Little Jim seemed to know exactly where he was going, however, and led them directly to the Power Rangers shelf. Once there he became totally absorbed, handling the figures with reverence.

Tanner stepped back from the display and pulled Dori with him. "I still can't believe he doesn't at least have that

White Ranger. It's his favorite character," he said, keeping his voice low.

"I can't afford it," she murmured. "The custody fight put me in a financial hole."

"I understand that, but what about his father and grandparents? I thought they were wealthy."

"And very dictatorial. They don't like the Power Ranger craze, maybe partly because I took Little Jim to the movie as a special treat last year, when I still had custody. They refuse to buy him anything to do with the Power Rangers."

"That's insane." Anger boiled up within Tanner as he watched Little Jim caress the figure of the White Ranger and put him gently back on the shelf. "He's just a little kid, for God's sake. Who do these people think they are?"

Dori gave him a sad smile. "The Devaneys."

"Well, they don't have dominion over me." Tanner stepped forward and crouched down next to Little Jim. "Pick out whatever you want on this shelf. I'll buy it for you." He had a moment to see the shock and joy register on Little Jim's face before Dori yanked him upright.

"No," she said, her dark gaze adamant. "Thank you, but no."

Tanner frowned at her display of pride. "He loves those characters. I can remember loving G.I. Joe the same way. I still have that stuff packed away somewhere. That's how we preserve a piece of our childhood, Dori. I can't believe you'd deny him that." He turned back to the boy. "Anything on the shelf. Pick it out."

Dori grabbed Tanner's arm. Her voice was low and intense. "Forget it, Tanner. He'll want it all. Do you know how much money that would be?"

"Less than dinner for two at a five-star restaurant," Tanner snapped, and immediately regretted it.

Dori's eyes widened. "And how would you know that?"

He stood mutely before her and wondered if he'd have to confess everything right now, before they'd had twenty-four hours together. He'd blown it, and all because he'd suddenly remembered the rush of joy when he'd become the proud owner of his first G.I. Joe figure. And if anybody needed that kind of joy in his confusing life, it was Little Jim.

"You've taken a date to a five-star restaurant, haven't you, Tanner?" Dori's expression was stormy.

"Yes." He waited for her to guess the rest of it. They hadn't built enough friendship between them, let alone love, for her to forgive his deception. Everything was ruined.

She braced her hands on her hips. "I can certainly see what your problem is. I suppose your credit cards are maxed out, aren't they?"

"Actually, I—"

"Never mind." She held up a hand. "We'll talk about it later. It's time to start home, anyway. Come on, Little Jim."

Her son looked ready to burst into tears. "I can't have anything?"

"Not today, sweetheart. But Christmas isn't so far away."

Tanner felt like a jerk. In his attempt to do something nice for the kid, he'd brought more stress into his young life. And although Dori hadn't guessed that Tanner was rich, she'd decided he was in debt. He didn't like that conclusion any better. He put a hand on Dori's arm. "Wait."

"Let's just get beyond this, okay?" she said gently. "We'll discuss it later."

"I'm not in debt. I—"

"I find that hard to believe."

"Please believe it. And let me buy at least one thing for Little Jim. I promise you it won't break the bank. And it means so much to him." Tanner was amazed that during the exchange Little Jim just stared up at them without saying a word. From Tanner's small store of knowledge about kids, he would have expected the boy to beg his mother for the toy. His silence was a tribute to Dori's careful teaching.

Dori glanced at her son. Then she crouched down so she was at eye level with him. "If I let Tanner buy you a present, don't expect that every time you see him you'll get something else. Tanner's in construction, like Grandpa Fitzpatrick, and he doesn't have the kind of money your daddy and your Grandma and Grandpa Devaney do. So this is a very, very special occasion. Can you remember that?"

As Little Jim nodded vigorously, Tanner felt worse and worse. What he'd thought to be an innocent subterfuge was turning into a gigantic misrepresentation. He'd once thought it would be easy to tell Dori the truth when the time came. Now he wasn't so sure. Ironically, everything Dori had said was true. Tanner didn't have the kind of money the Devaneys had. He had much more.

6

Tanner offered to drive home, and Dori took him up on it. She didn't trust herself to concentrate on the road, considering the disturbing thoughts chasing themselves around in her mind.

While Little Jim played happily with the White Ranger in the back seat and Tanner dealt with the heavier traffic that usually hit the stretch between Abilene and Los Lobos at five o'clock, Dori sorted through her limited options. She couldn't let herself become involved with a spendthrift. She'd seen that mentality a thousand times in people with sporadic paychecks. When the money came in, they spent lavishly until it was gone, giving no thought to budgeting for the lean times. Her mother and father had taught her how to avoid that trap. When she'd married Jimmy Jr., she'd thought that particular survival skill wouldn't be necessary anymore. Now it was her lifeline.

If she married again and began another campaign to get custody of Little Jim, she'd need every penny to pay her lawyer. A man who allowed money to dribble through his fingers would be more of a liability than an asset. Not that she didn't understand the impulse that had driven Tanner to suggest buying out the toy store. She'd had the same impulse many times in her desire to make up for her son's suffering. Tanner was a soft-hearted guy who was new to the situation and perhaps overspending should be forgiven.

Yet it seemed that extravagance was a pattern with him. Twice, he'd demonstrated in her presence that he wasn't careful with money, and he'd admitted taking a date to a restaurant way beyond his means. Dori kept trying to think about that, when all she wanted to think about was his kiss, his strong arms holding her close, his body becoming aroused. . . .

The night before she'd vowed not to be blinded by sexual attraction. And she wouldn't be. Before she got in any deeper, she'd ask Tanner to leave. She simply couldn't take the chance of making another gigantic mistake.

"Momma!" Little Jim shook her shoulder.

Dori snapped out of her trance with a guilty start and turned toward the back seat. "What, sweetheart?"

"I was calling you and calling you, but you didn't hear me."

"Sorry. I was thinking." She noticed the movement as Tanner glanced at her. He knew she was worried about that scene in the store.

"You're always thinking," Little Jim complained.

"I suppose I am." She managed a smile. His Dallas Cowboys cap was crammed down tight on his head to keep it from blowing off in the wind, and he had to peer up at her from under the bill of the cap. He clutched the White Ranger in a death grip. Dori suspected he'd sleep with the action figure and hoped none of the Devaneys would give him a hard time about the new toy. "What did you want to say?" she asked.

"Can you make me a White Ranger costume for Halloween?"

"Hold him up and let me look."

Little Jim raised the figure cautiously from his lap. "Just don't want him to blow out," he explained.

Dori studied the Power Ranger's outfit and estimated how much fabric it would take, and how much skill. Thank goodness for her mother's old sewing machine. "I think I can manage that," she said.

"O*kay!* Wait'll Jerry and Melissa and Stanley see me!"

Dori felt the familiar tug of regret. He didn't spend much time with his neighborhood playmates anymore and she knew he missed them. "I . . . I'm not sure you'll be going trick-or-treating with them this year, sweetheart."

"Why not?"

"Halloween's on a Thursday."

Little Jim seemed to absorb that news. "I have to go there. We don't have any houses around Grandpa and Grandma Devaney's."

"We'll see. I'll talk to them about it."

"Will Tanner be here on Halloween?"

"Oh, I don't think so, honey," Dori answered. "He has to get back to Dallas soon."

"Will he be here next Monday?"

"No, he won't, sweetheart." She glanced at Tanner. He'd suggested spending approximately a week in Los Lobos, although they'd both known the time could be shortened if the relationship didn't seem to be working.

He took his eyes from traffic long enough to meet her gaze. "I plan to still be here next Monday," he said as he returned his attention to the road.

Dori worked to get her racing heart under control. In one brief glance, Tanner had managed to convey an intensity of desire that swept away her latest resolution and left thudding passion in its wake. Suddenly the money issue seemed unimportant, even petty, compared to the searing force of that look. Dori struggled to remain rational, but she was at war with a body that demanded the very thing Tanner had silently promised to give. Still, she had to send him away, no matter how much she wanted him.

Tanner spoke over his shoulder to Little Jim. "Any objection if I hang around until Monday?"

"I guess not," Little Jim said.

"Thanks."

Dori evaluated Tanner's grim smile and concluded he wasn't satisfied with her son's lukewarm answer. Maybe he thought buying the White Ranger should have made them friends for life. If so, he was in for a rude awakening. Little Jim's affections couldn't be bought, and neither could his mother. Not even with potent kisses and melting looks.

A few minutes later Tanner flicked on the turn signal for the exit to Los Lobos. Dori had two more hours before she was scheduled to take Little Jim home, and she wanted to spend them alone with her son. She directed Tanner to the motel, and he drove there without comment.

In front of the motel, she got out and climbed into the driver's seat of the convertible as Tanner held the door.

He closed it firmly and rested both hands on the door-frame as he gazed down at her. "We need to talk."

"Yes, we do. I'll drop my son off at eight. I can come by after that, if it's not too late."

"Not at all." He straightened. "Oh, it's room nine."

She lifted a startled gaze to his. "You're kidding."

"Nope."

"Nine is Momma's lucky number," Little Jim chimed in from the back seat.

"So I hear."

Dori still couldn't believe it. "Out of twenty-seven rooms in this motel, you're in number nine. That's incredible."

"Isn't it?"

"Well, we'd better get going." She turned toward the back seat. "Come on, son." As he made his way between the bucket seats and plopped down, she touched his shoulder. "Thank Tanner for your gift."

"Thank you, Tanner," Little Jim said. "I really like him."

"That's good. I'll see you next Monday, buddy."

"Okay."

Dori waved and pulled out of the parking lot. Room number nine. She really couldn't believe it. Maybe she was tempting fate to doubt that this was the right man for her. Maybe she should give him just a little longer to prove it one way or the other.

WHEN THE CONVERTIBLE was out of sight, Tanner headed straight for the motel office. Elmer wasn't there. Behind the front desk stood a white-haired, matronly woman whose name tag read Beatrice. Tanner guessed she might be Elmer's wife.

Apparently, she knew all about Tanner, because she smiled when he walked in. "Mr. Jones, isn't it?"

"That's right."

"Elmer told me you were here. You're in room sixteen, aren't you? I trust you had a pleasant night?"

AFTER DORI DROVE BACK to her house, she fixed Little Jim his favorite dinner of toasted cheese sandwiches and they played slapjack until it was time for him to go back to the Devaneys. Those last few minutes as they rushed around gathering Little Jim's belongings were usually the hardest for Dori. She always saved the packet of the previous week's pictures to tuck into his knapsack just before they walked out the door of the house they used to share. Little Jim hoarded them for when he was alone in his room, so he'd still have his mother's face to look at.

Normally on the short drive to the Devaney mansion, Little Jim was subdued, but tonight he had questions. "Do you like Tanner, Momma?"

She hesitated, thinking about Tanner's habit of tossing money around. Although it was a big worry, it was the only negative she'd found. Otherwise he'd shown himself to be courageous, gallant, sensitive . . . and sexy. "Yes, I like him," she said.

"Better than Daddy?"

Absolutely, she thought, but she couldn't say that. "Your daddy has some fine qualities," she forced herself to say. "But we just don't see things the same."

"Do you see things the same as Tanner?"

Dori took a deep breath. "I don't know yet. That's what I'm trying to find out."

"Why?"

She couldn't tell Little Jim her long-range plan. He was too young to understand the plotting she'd done in an attempt to get him back. "Well, someday I'd like to get married again," she said. "But I want to make sure the man is somebody I like a lot, and somebody you like a lot, too."

"Daddy says you're gonna marry him again."

Dori silently cursed Jimmy Jr. for confiding his fantasies to their son. "When did he say that?"

"Oh, he says it all the time. He says then we can all be together again."

She clenched her jaw. Jimmy was shameless. "I'm afraid that's not going to happen, sweetheart."

"Couldn't you *try* to like Daddy?"

Dori turned down the winding road to the mansion, her stomach in knots. "Sometimes all the trying in the world won't work. Remember when I read that article about tofu?"

"Yeah, I sure do!"

"But I kept thinking if I cooked it a different way, or with different food, we'd learn to like it. We really tried, didn't we?"

"I hated that yucky tofu."

Dori braked the car. No lights shone from the front windows, so everyone must be in the back of the house, she thought. Even at night the house didn't look welcoming. "But some people like tofu fine," she continued. "I just gave up trying."

"Daddy's like tofu?"

"Yep. For me he is."

Little Jim sat quite still as he seemed to turn the concept over in his mind. Then he looked up at her. "If Daddy's tofu, what's Tanner?"

A hot fudge sundae. "I'm not sure yet. We have to get better acquainted." Finally, she asked the most important question, knowing she'd been putting it off until the last moment. "What do you think of him?"

Little Jim stared out the windshield into the darkness. "He's okay. But—"

"But?"

"But I sure wish Daddy wasn't tofu," he said softly.

Dori reached an arm around him and gave him a squeeze. "So do I."

She walked him up the steps and rang the bell. If she was lucky Crystal would answer the door again. She wasn't lucky. Jimmy Jr. opened the door and gazed out at them.

Little Jim did what most five-year-olds would have, and held up his new toy. "See, Daddy? The White Ranger!"

Jimmy frowned. "Your momma must be feelin' flush if she's buying you stuff."

"Tanner bought it," Little Jim said. Then he glanced into his father's face and cringed.

"You went with that ol' boy to Abilene?" Jimmy demanded. "After I told you not to?"

"But Momma said—"

"Your momma has taken leave of her senses. Give me that stupid toy."

Dori stepped in front of Little Jim to shield him. "You're not depriving him of that toy, Jimmy. If he can't keep it here, then I'll take it home with me, to have for him when he comes over."

"Don't be telling me what I can and can't do with my own son! Your time's up, Dori Mae. What happens with him is my business now."

"What's going on here?" James Devaney strode into the hallway, the light from the back of the house surrounding him. A good two inches taller than his son, with a lean, tanned face and a full head of silver hair, he had the sort of manner that made people step back in deference.

His son was no exception. As Jimmy moved away from the door, he motioned to Dori and Little Jim. "She had a date with that construction worker today and dragged my son along."

James lifted an eyebrow in obvious disapproval as he glanced at Jimmy Jr. "So you make things worse by causing a commotion out here on the front porch, like some poor white trash. And in front of the boy, too. You should both be ashamed of yourselves."

Behind her back, Dori motioned for Little Jim to give her the White Ranger. It wasn't safe in this house, and they both knew it now. Little Jim put the White Ranger into her hand slowly, keeping his own grip on it as long as possible.

"I'll be running along," Dori said, keeping the figure behind her as she backed toward the steps. "See you next Monday, Little Jim."

"Bye, Momma." He tried manfully not to cry, but his lower lip quivered.

Dori trembled with fury. She could guess what it cost him to give up his beloved White Ranger, but she figured it would land in the trash compactor if she hadn't taken it. That would be worse.

"Come on, L.J.," James said, putting his hand on Little Jim's shoulder. "I think Grandma has some cookies for you." As he guided the child away, he glanced back at Jimmy. "Cut it short. This is not the time or place."

Jimmy glared back at his father but didn't reply. Dori knew he was too aware of his own interests to risk crossing the man who wrote out his paycheck. Unlike his older sister, who'd finally had enough and had fled to California, Jimmy seemed willing to bide his time until he could be in charge. At which time, Dori had no doubt, he'd behave exactly as his father did. In the meantime, he'd expected to have Dori to boss around. She'd cheated him of that opportunity, and he didn't like it.

"I warned you to get that ol' boy out of town," Jimmy said in a low voice.

Dori eased down the steps, careful not to let him see the toy in her hand. "Good night, Jimmy."

"I warned you," he said again.

She reached the car and got in quickly. As she drove away, the White Ranger in her lap, she checked her rearview mirror. She kept checking all the way to the Prairie Schooner Motel. But even if Jimmy didn't follow her there, he'd eventually find out where she'd gone. People in Los Lobos kept track of each other by noticing where vehicles were parked. Everybody in town knew her white Sunbird convertible. Too bad she hadn't chosen a more ordinary car, but it couldn't be helped now. She'd promised to have a talk with Tanner. She wouldn't stay long.

WHEN THE SOFT KNOCK CAME at the door, Tanner switched off the television and leapt from the bed where he'd been sprawling, the pillows shoved behind his head. His heart pounded in anticipation of whether this would be her kiss-off speech. He sure as hell hoped not, but she'd been angry about his offer to buy all those Power Ranger things, and he'd been a fool to suggest it.

Telling her he was in room nine had been an inspiration. And his luck had held, because nine hadn't been rented out yet and he was able to convince Beatrice to let him switch by making up some story about the television not working right. Before he'd moved out of sixteen he'd screwed up the controls enough to give Elmer something to do when he went to check out the set later. Elmer had reported to him that nothing was wrong with the set except that somebody had messed with the settings, but by that time Tanner had taken possession of room nine.

He opened the door and restrained himself from gathering her immediately into his arms. Instead, he stepped back and allowed her to walk past him into the room. Then he noticed that she held the White Ranger in one hand. His stomach clenched. She was about to deliver the kiss-off speech, complete with the return of his gift to her son.

He closed the door and turned to her. Desperation made him reckless.

"Tanner, I—"

"Don't." He closed the gap between them and pulled her into his arms. He'd told himself not to use Neanderthal tactics, but the specter of losing her canceled his good intentions. In the middle of her startled exclamation of surprise he brought his mouth down on hers. If she fought him, he'd let her go.

She didn't fight. She caught fire. Her shoulder purse slid to the floor and the White Ranger's leg pressed into his shoulder as she wound her arms around his neck. He didn't care. Nothing mattered except the urgency of her mouth inviting him to delve inside and possess her. His thrusting tongue presented a blatant suggestion of the more complete union he sought. Cupping her bottom, he brought her tight against his arousal, wanting her to know exactly how she was affecting him. His pulse raced as she wiggled even closer, and he groaned at the perfect way they fit together.

He pulled the hem of her T-shirt from her jeans and reached beneath it to unfasten her bra. Before he could accomplish it, she shoved him away.

"Not yet," she gasped.

His voice was husky with need. "Why not? We're both ready for it, Dori."

She waited until her breathing slowed before answering. "Physically, perhaps. Not mentally. I hope you didn't think, because I offered to come to your room, that I was giving you permission to sleep with me."

"No, I didn't think that." He couldn't keep the impatience from his voice. "But after the way you responded when I kissed you just now, I thought the time had arrived."

"You caught me by surprise, is all. I wasn't expecting you to grab me like that, and it was . . ." She glanced up at him through her lashes. "Exciting." Her endearing habit of drawing out the letter *i* gave a whole new emphasis to the word.

He swallowed. "No kidding."

"But I really came here to talk."

"And return Little Jim's gift?"

She glanced down at the figure in her hand as if she'd forgotten she was holding it. "Oh! No, I just brought this in because the top's still down on the car and somebody might take it. I could have used the glove compartment or the trunk, I suppose, but bringing it in was the easiest thing to do." She laid the figure on the bed and reached behind her to tuck in her T-shirt where he'd pulled it out.

If the gesture was meant to discourage Tanner from trying to kiss her again, it did. "How come Little Jim doesn't have his toy?"

Her eyes darkened. "I was afraid somebody in that house would destroy it."

"Destroy a kid's toy?" The idea left a bitter taste in his mouth. "What kind of people are they?"

"They'd make it look like an accident, but I could see by the expression on Jimmy's face, and even his father's, that they'd get rid of it. I told you they didn't want him playing with Power Ranger stuff. He gets the toys they want him to have. Some of them are very expensive, but he doesn't have any choice in the matter. They control his life completely."

"That's sick."

"That's why I want him back."

He looked into her eyes. It could all be so easy, so quick. He could tell her about his thriving business and ask her to marry him. His lawyers would make mincemeat of the Devaneys, and Little Jim would be reunited with his mother. But Tanner couldn't forget her speech about carelessly throwing up a house and hoping the structure was solid instead of taking the time to do it right. She'd already put Little Jim through one divorce. He knew she didn't want to risk a second one. They'd have to do this her way.

"I should warn you about Jimmy Jr.," she said. "He came to the door and wasn't pleased about you going along to Abilene with me and Little Jim. He might try something."

"And he might be all talk."

"He might. I doubt he'd ever take you on man-to-man."

"No. He's a certified bully."

Dori shoved her hands in the front pockets of her jeans and stared down at her running shoes. "That's what worries me. He won't challenge you to a fair fight, but he might talk some of his buddies into waylaying you sometime when you're alone." She glanced up, her expression troubled. "I don't want you to get hurt, Tanner. Maybe it would be best if you gave up on me."

"We've already had this discussion. You're wasting your time trying to convince me to leave, unless you want me to go for your own reasons. But I refuse to run away from Jimmy's threats."

Admiration shone from her eyes. "You're almost perfect, you know that?"

There. That was what he'd been searching for all these years, a woman who looked at him, not at what he represented in material perks, and was impressed. "I'm far from perfect, but I'm glad you think I'm even close."

"The one bad thing is the way you spend money, Tanner. I couldn't tolerate that in a husband."

"I can change."

She smiled. "I'm glad you said that, because I've thought of a way to help you. Here's my plan. For the next week, if you agree, you'll be on a budget."

"A what?"

She looked a trifle smug, but on Dori the expression was cute. "I figured you weren't closely acquainted with that concept. Here's how it would work. Whatever we do together all week has to cost less than the total I've come up with."

He already knew he'd hate this. "And what is that total, pray tell?"

She walked over to the desk and picked up the pad and pen left there for guests. She wrote a figure on the pad, ripped off the page and handed it to him.

He stared at the small amount, less than it would cost him to dry-clean one of his custom suits. "No way."

"It can be done. You just have to use your imagination instead of your wallet. That's my condition, Tanner. Unless I truly believe you can be more careful with money, we have no future together. We should end it now before we both get hurt."

He looked at the amount and considered once more spilling the beans. Then he gazed at her standing in the circle of light created by the desk lamp. Her braid had loosened during the day, giving her a wonderfully disheveled look that he longed to improve upon. He recalled the promise in her kiss, the press of her ripe body, and could think of one thing they could do that would cost nothing at all.

"It's a deal," he said.

"Good." She took the paper back and drew a crude map on the back. "Here's how you get to my house." She handed him the paper before picking up her purse and the White Ranger. "You can come by for me at nine tomorrow morning. I don't have to be at work until one. Good night, Tanner."

He watched her head for the door. He wanted to call her back, yet knew she wouldn't stay the night, which was what he really wanted. "Thanks for giving me a second chance," he said.

She opened the door and stopped, turning to look back at him. "I thought about calling everything off, but when you told me you were in room nine, I figured that was a sign we should hang on a while longer."

After she left, Tanner shook his head. Talk about close calls.

7

TANNER WASN'T SLEEPING as well as usual since he arrived in Los Lobos. Sexual frustration could do that to a person, he'd discovered. He'd finally drifted off about one in the morning when the sound of yelling and people running brought him wide-awake. He pulled on his jeans and boots and opened his door, expecting to see flames leaping from one of the motel rooms.

The sidewalk in front of the long row of rooms was crowded with guests in various stages of undress, so that Tanner had a hard time figuring out where the problem originated. He moved out into the parking lot for a better perspective, which was when the breeze blew the stench in his direction. He coughed and held his breath as he studied the row of open doors and noticed wispy smoke drifting from room sixteen.

A cowboy ambled over to him, buttoning his shirt as he walked. "Smells like somebody threw a stink bomb in that room," he commented to Tanner. "Probably high school kids."

"Could be." Tanner breathed through his mouth as the smell became worse. He didn't think for a minute it was high school kids, despite the juvenile nature of the vandalism.

"Aren't you that ol' boy from East Texas that's here to see Dori?"

Tanner gazed at him, not feeling particularly friendly at the moment. "Who wants to know?"

The man stuck out his hand. "Heck Tyrrell, a friend of Dori's. I stop in at the Double Nickel whenever I'm in town."

Tanner shook his hand. "Tanner Jones."

"I know. I was there Sunday night. I made a run to Amarillo yesterday, but now my rig's in the shop until tomorrow afternoon, so I'm bunking here."

Tanner grew wary. "So you work for Devaney Trucking?"

"Yeah." Tyrrell rubbed his neck and looked uncomfortable. "A man's gotta have a job, and Devaney pays good."

"I understand."

Tyrrell hesitated, then spoke again. "Listen, Dori's something special. We don't want to see her get hurt."

"Seems like she's already been hurt."

Tyrrell looked down the road, where a wailing siren and flashing red lights indicated a fire truck was on the way. "Somebody shoulda punched Jimmy Jr. a long time ago," he said quietly.

"Probably."

"Treat her right, Jones."

"I intend to."

As the fire truck pulled in, Tanner excused himself from Tyrrell and headed back to his room. Room number nine. Dori's lucky number had saved him from some inconvenient nastiness.

THE NEXT MORNING Dori dressed in jeans and a San Antonio Spurs T-shirt her parents had sent her. With the budget she'd put Tanner on, he wouldn't be taking her anywhere fancy. She smiled as she remembered the look of disbelief that had crossed his handsome face when she'd set a limit on the amount he could spend on her in the next week. She'd half expected him to refuse to abide by her budget and was very glad he'd decided to go along. Apparently, he understood the importance of proving he could be thrifty.

And someday she might tell him how tough it had been for her to walk out of his motel room after the way he'd kissed her. Keeping him at arm's length while she evaluated his suitability as a husband and father was the most difficult thing she'd ever had to do. But she would continue with that course of action for Little Jim's sake.

After some inner debate, she left her freshly washed hair loose. She didn't wear it that way often because she was either working at the café or puttering around her house, and unbound hair got in the way. Besides, Dori had always thought when a woman let her hair flow loose around her shoulders, she was signaling an interest in romance. Dori hadn't wanted to give off those signals. Until now.

Her doorbell rang at precisely nine, and she marked down punctuality on her mental list of Tanner's good qualities. The list was growing. If he could just learn to budget . . .

She pulled open the door and forgot all about the spending habits of the man standing on her tiny front porch. Dressed in a soft blue work shirt and snug jeans, Tanner looked even better than he had in the *Texas Men* magazine photo, and that was saying a lot. Or maybe her perception of him was beginning to shift as memories of passionate kisses colored her view.

From behind his back, he produced a Hershey chocolate bar and a single white carnation. "Bargain candy, bargain flower in virginal white, signifying my pure intentions," he said with a wink. "Do I have to save my receipts, or will you keep this all in your head?"

She laughed and accepted the candy bar and carnation. "After two years of watching every penny, I'll know when you've crossed the line. Thank you. This is very nice." She stepped back and ushered him inside.

"Let me have the flower back," he said as she closed the door.

"What, you're going to recycle it for tomorrow? That may be going a bit far, Tanner."

"You'll get it back in a minute." He slipped the carnation from her fingers and snapped off a good part of the stem.

"Hey! That's my present you're mutilating."

"I just found out where it goes." He moved closer and tucked the carnation in her hair. The delicate scent of the flower mingled in a heady combination with his woodsy after-shave, and his breath fell softly on her face as he concentrated on getting the flower anchored behind her ear. "There." His tone had undergone a subtle change, from bantering to husky, and his hand lingered on her cheek.

She looked up into his eyes and could read intentions that were far from pure. Her pulse raced.

With a rueful smile he backed away. "Sorry. Almost forgot myself for a minute."

She was impressed with his self-control. And perhaps a little disappointed. Which was very unfair of her, she realized.

He glanced down at her hand. "You're going to melt the candy bar, holding it like that."

Immediately, she relaxed her death grip on the Hershey bar.

"Gonna give me a tour of your house?"

"Sure. Let's go back to the kitchen first. I'll put the candy in the fridge." Her legs a bit rubbery, she led him to the kitchen, a long, narrow room with her refinished round oak table at one end, a closet for her secondhand washer and dryer at the other. The kitchen window looked out on the backyard, where Little Jim's swing set and a picnic table took up most of the area. A red oak, an unusual tree for the area, shaded the picnic table. The leaves had begun to turn and a few had fluttered down to make bright scarlet patches on the grass. The tree had captured Little Jim's imagination and Dori had rented the house because her son loved that tree.

Tanner braced his hands on the sink and peered out the window at the view over the cedar fence that surrounded the yard. He stared at the large two-story house about a mile away, where an upstairs window was visible in a break between the branches of the large cottonwoods that surrounded the house like sentinels. Tanner glanced over his shoulder at Dori. "Little Jim's room?"

"That's right. If those trees grow any more, I won't be able to see it."

Tanner looked back at the house. "Let's hope you don't have to worry about that."

Longing filled her heart as she imagined having this broad-shouldered man beside her, helping her fight what seemed like an impossible battle. A sigh must have escaped unnoticed, because he turned around, concern in his eyes.

"Let's drop that depressing subject," he said. "You spend enough time worrying, as it is." He winked. "Let's go see the rest of the house. I want to find out if you've put a velvet rope across the door to your bedroom."

"You really think I'm prissy, don't you?"

"No, I think you're sexy as hell, and if I don't crack jokes I'm liable to grab you and try to seduce you, which would spoil everything, right?"

She found breathing difficult. "Right," she whispered.

"Then let's get on with the tour."

"Right," she said again, and walked ahead of him out of the kitchen. This plan had seemed so logical when she'd written to Tanner suggesting he come to Los Lobos for a week so they could get acquainted. But the sexual tug she felt every time she looked at him had nothing to do with logic.

She led him back through the living room toward the hall.

"You've been very creative with your decorating, by the way," he said as they passed through the living room.

"You have to be creative when you're on a budget."

"So I'm learning."

She walked down the hall and paused before Little Jim's room, which looked pretty much as he'd left it six months ago. His yard-sale toy box sat in one corner and his twin bed held the assortment of stuffed animals he'd collected since he was a baby. "My son's room, obviously," she said. "Jimmy Jr. thought Little Jim was too big for stuffed animals, so he left them all here. He left most of his other toys, too." She didn't admit that sometimes, when the ache for her son was too much to bear, she slept here surrounded by his cherished bears, squirrels and bunnies. Little Jim's scent clung to the soft toys, and breathing it in helped her sleep.

Tanner glanced into the room but made no comment.

"I suppose he is too old for stuffed animals," Dori said.

"Nobody ever gets that old, Dori. The way your ex-husband treats Little Jim chills my blood."

She glanced into his eyes and drew strength from the anger there. "Jimmy always told me I didn't know anything about raising boys."

"That's ridiculous. I've seen what you've done with that boy, and you know everything you need to know. He's a great kid."

A smile trembled on her lips. "Thanks, Tanner. Hearing that helps a lot. You know, I think if Little Jim had been a girl, the judge would have ruled differently, thinking girls need their mothers more. God help me, I've sometimes wished Little Jim had been a girl so I wouldn't have lost my child."

His gaze grew more intense as she talked. "Dammit, why don't we just—" Abruptly he stopped speaking and turned away with a muted curse.

"What?"

He faced her again, his expression more placid. "Never mind. Let's continue the tour."

"Okay." She could guess what he'd been thinking. The talk about Little Jim had brought him back to the idea of a quickie marriage in Las Vegas. Fortunately, he'd thought better of bringing up the subject again. "This is my room." She gestured toward the door. "Bathroom's across the hall."

She stood back and let Tanner look in. He did a double take at the pictures of her son that covered all four walls.

"I had a lot of pictures, because Little Jim is the only grandchild on both sides. When he . . . went to live with the Devaneys, I hauled them all out and tacked them up. Then we take pictures every week, as you saw yesterday. Rolls of film are one extravagance I allow myself."

Tanner stood silently examining the walls full of pictures. Finally, he turned back to her, a grim set to his jaw. "Let's go," he said, his voice strained. "We have a house to build."

He wouldn't tell her where they were headed when he guided her out the door and into his truck, but she saw what appeared to be a picnic basket in the back.

"You won't get us lost, will you?" she asked as they took off down a back road.

He grinned at her. "Worried about being stranded with me in some lonely spot?"

The idea filled her with more excitement than she dared tell him. "I just meant you don't know the area very well."

"No, but Elmer does. I spent some time talking to him this morning before I picked you up."

He seemed so proud of himself, taking her out for an inexpensive picnic, that she hated to rain directly on his parade, so she chose a more oblique approach. "I'm surprised Hanson's Department Store was open this morning."

"Hanson's?" He glanced at her. "What do you mean?"

She angled her head back toward the truck bed. "Isn't that where you bought the picnic basket?"

"Oh." He nodded. "A picnic basket would blow the budget right off, wouldn't it?"

"I'm afraid so, Tanner. But still, it's a great idea. You have a handicap, being from out of town and all. You don't have a lot of the things you might otherwise."

"I hate to tell you, but even if we were in East Texas, I'd be out of luck. I don't own a picnic basket."

"Well, now you do."

"No, I don't."

"But—"

"I borrowed it from Elmer's wife, Beatrice."

Dori chuckled at his self-righteous expression. "That's great, Tanner."

"I'll be darned if she didn't have the whole works—tablecloth, silverware, plastic plates and glasses. The only thing I paid for was the food, and she helped me make the sandwiches in her kitchen."

"I'm impressed." She was also touched. Tanner had taken her so seriously that he'd befriended the motel owners and asked for their help. She suspected Tanner wasn't used to asking people for special favors. "So you've made friends with Beatrice, then?"

He drove with one hand on the steering wheel, the other resting on the floor shift. "I think you're the reason she was so helpful."

"Me?" She found herself staring at his shift hand only a few inches from her knee. The Texas sun had burnished his skin, and there was a small scratch near his thumb that had nearly healed. His fingers curved lazily over the shift knob, and she could see that his nails were short and clean. It was a working hand, probably scratched by a rough piece of board or a wayward screwdriver. And she wanted to feel the caress of that capable hand on her skin.

"I get the idea that a lot of people in Los Lobos would like to see you break free of Jimmy Jr.'s domination," he said. "They just can't be too vocal about it."

Dori sighed, as much to release sexual tension as anything. "I know. I've had some great support from a couple of old high school friends. They're the ones who advised me to get married again. They were all set to help me find somebody, but then I saw the magazine and decided to try that, first."

Quietly, smoothly, Tanner moved his hand from the gearshift and laced his fingers through hers. "I'm glad."

Desire jolted through her at the subtle pressure of those strong fingers. She took a deep breath. "You know, we have to remember something."

The corner of his mouth lifted. "Tell me and I'll add it to the list."

"We might not get Little Jim back. We could get married, and pay the lawyer a lot of money, and still not get him."

"We would get him."

He spoke with such complete confidence that she wanted to take his word for it, but that was being naive. "You don't know the power the Devaneys have down here. The judge who heard the case last time had known

James Devaney for thirty years. Like I said, we might not get him."

Tanner was silent for a moment. "And what would you do then?"

She honestly hadn't thought that far.

"Because if you'd divorce me and go back to Jimmy, just so you could be with Little Jim, you'd better tell me now."

"That would be horrible!"

"I agree. Would you do it?"

She thought about it, knowing that whatever her answer, it would have to be the final one. As recently as Sunday night she'd contemplated going back to Jimmy as a last resort. But now, with Tanner's hand holding hers, that seemed like a sin against herself that she could not commit, not even to be with her son.

"No," she said. "No, I wouldn't divorce you and go back to Jimmy."

His grip on her hand relaxed a fraction. "That's good to know," he said mildly, but there was a note of underlying tension.

"I'd want to keep trying to get Little Jim, though," she said.

"Of course. We'd never give up."

A lump lodged in her throat. That was what she'd needed to know. She remained silent until she trusted herself to speak again. "Tell me about your family," she said at last.

As he complied, she worked to keep details in mind, when what she really wanted was to hold him close and thank him for being the kind of man she'd dreamed about all her life. She managed to retain information about a younger sister struggling with the rigors of law school and parents who lived a comfortable but unpretentious life in Illinois.

Most important of all, Dori sensed the love that had surrounded Tanner as he grew up. Perhaps his devoted parents had indulged him a few times too often, which would explain his readiness to spend money without considering the consequences. But she'd rather deal with that problem than a lack of love, which tended to warp people in a way that was hard to straighten.

"Does your family know you came down here to meet me?" she asked.

"Yeah." Tanner laughed. "My mother couldn't understand why I needed to advertise for a wife, considering that I'm such a wonderful catch."

"You are, Tanner."

He took his attention from the road to glance at her in amusement. "As long as I learn some financial restraint, right?"

She nodded.

He returned his gaze to the road and rubbed his thumb across the back of her hand. "Financial restraint won't be the tough part."

As Dori's body warmed in response, she had to agree.

Tanner took a left turn on a dirt road. Driving slow enough that he kept the dust from billowing around them, he headed for a stand of cottonwoods. Dori had forgotten about this little oasis in the mostly treeless flatland around Los Lobos, although she'd come here a few times as a child. A rare underground spring fed the spot, creating a small pond that encouraged the cottonwoods to grow. This time of year, they shone yellow as ripe corn in the sunlight.

Dori smiled. "Trust you to seek out the only trees around for miles."

"I know how you like the open sky, but picnics and trees seem to go together. Elmer told me about Abilene Lake, but it would have taken longer to get there and we wouldn't have been alone."

Dori's heart pounded. "Which might have been a good thing."

Leaves crunched under the tires as Tanner guided the truck off the roadway and found a shady place to park. He switched off the engine and turned to her. "I said my intentions were pure. I never promised not to kiss you. And I prefer kissing in private."

Her heart pounded faster. "Just kissing?"

He regarded her with a twinkle in his eyes. "You sound disappointed."

"No! I just . . . wanted us to be clear."

His gaze became more serious. "We're clear." Then he opened his door. "Come on. We have to start back in less than two hours."

Dori helped him spread the red gingham tablecloth over a bed of fallen leaves and unpack the lunch. In the cottonwood tree above them a pair of canyon wrens sent their shimmering call down through the gold leaves. Little Jim would have loved this outing, she thought. Then she experienced a flash of guilt because she was secretly glad her son wasn't with them today. With a start she realized that being with Tanner eased the grief of not having Little Jim with her. That was important, considering there were no guarantees about making this group a threesome in the future.

"You do know about poison ivy, don't you?" she asked as Tanner set the basket in the middle of the cloth and opened it.

He glanced toward a scarlet-leaved plant about twenty feet away. "Like that?"

"Like that. Years ago one of my cousins visiting from Arizona brought me a bouquet of fall leaves. He was especially proud of the bright red ones. He had a miserable visit after that."

Tanner laughed. "Poor guy. Did you have him on a budget, too?"

"For your information, I am not in the habit of putting people on budgets. In fact, I've never done it before."

He sat back on his heels and gazed at her. "I guess that puts me in a special category."

"I guess it does."

He grinned. "Shoot, anything to stand out from the crowd, I always say. Let's eat."

Tanner's choice for lunch was ham sandwiches, chips, lemonade and a package of chocolate cupcakes. They sat on either side of the picnic basket, plates balanced on their laps and their lemonade glasses sitting on the closed lid of the basket as they ate.

"The sandwiches are delicious," Dori said after enjoying her first bite.

"Thanks. I haven't made sandwiches in a long time, but I guess it's not the sort of thing you forget how to do."

"You eat out a lot, don't you?"

"Yep." He bit a big chunk from his sandwich.

"That's wasteful, Tanner."

He finished chewing and swallowed before glancing sideways at her. "Maybe I was compensating for not having someone like you sitting across from me."

"There you go again, with that sweet talk."

"Want me to stop?"

"No. I'm truly beginning to enjoy it." She watched an orange dragonfly dip toward the small pond, take on water and buzz skyward again like a miniature biplane dusting crops. "You know, I haven't shared a picnic lunch with a man since . . ." She paused and reached into her memory. "Since high school, I guess. And back then my dates were technically boys, not men. So I guess I've never had a picnic with a man unless you count my daddy."

"Did you ever come out here?"

She finished a bite of sandwich. "Not on dates. We always went to Abilene Lake. But my momma and daddy brought me out here when I was younger than Little Jim." She glanced at the pond, not much bigger than her backyard. "They teased me about that picnic for years afterward. It seems that when I saw the water, I asked Daddy if this was the ocean."

Tanner chuckled.

"I hadn't traveled much. In fact, when I married Jimmy Jr., I still hadn't been very many places. We went to Hawaii on our honeymoon and I just stared at that amazing water. All the different colors just knocked me out."

"It's spectacular, all right."

"You've been there?" She gazed at him and shook her head. "I'm really worried about you. Champagne tastes on a beer budget, as they say. You have to live within your means if you're not rich like the Devaneys."

He set aside his plate. "Reform me."

Her pulse quickened at the look in his eyes. "I'm trying. But Hawaii, Tanner! You're going to be a hard case."

"Maybe I didn't have anything better to do." He lifted the picnic basket, careful not to spill the lemonade, and settled it at the far edge of the tablecloth. Then he took her plate from her unresisting hands and set it on the top of the basket. "Going to Hawaii was the most exciting thing I could think of."

Her breathing grew shallow as he leaned toward her, the promise of a kiss in his intense gaze. Balanced on one outstretched hand, she met him halfway. "Didn't anyone ever tell you that the best things in life are free?" she whispered.

"I didn't really believe it." He paused a fraction away from the kiss. "Until I met you."

Only their lips touched, withdrew and touched again, almost as if they'd choreographed the delicate movement required. Too much pressure by either of them would send one of them toppling. Too little would mute the satisfaction of tasting each other. His tongue questioned, hers answered. Then, as she began to tremble and lose her balance, he caught her shoulders and guided her down, his mouth never leaving hers.

Beneath them the leaves crunched. Dori accepted Tanner's weight with a sigh of delight and wound her arms around him, bringing him closer. She'd forgotten the delicious feeling of a man lying against her breasts, exerting just enough pressure to knead their fullness with his movements.

He lifted his head to gaze down at her, but kept her lightly pinned to the gingham cloth with his upper body. Slowly he combed her hair with his fingers, his eyes alight with pleasure. "You wore your hair down. Was that for me?"

"Yes."

His glance roamed over her face. "You were made for this season of the year. The red in your hair . . ." He buried his fingers in it before leaning in close again. "The little gold flecks in your eyes when the sun's just right." He ran the tip of his finger over her parted lips. "And your mouth is the color of ripe apples."

"Sweet talker." She cupped the back of his head. "Kiss me again, Tanner. Kiss me real good."

His mouth came down again, hungrier now, but so was she. This time when he pulled her T-shirt from the waistband of her jeans and reached for the back catch of her bra, she arched her back to allow him to do it. And at last those workman's hands she'd fantasized about were cupping her breasts, stroking her nipples, making her whimper with desire.

It was heaven on earth, but she couldn't let him go on and think her a tease. She grasped his hands, holding on tight, and his movements stilled. He raised his head and gazed down at her. Silently, she looked into his eyes and watched the resignation settle in their blue depths. Slowly, he helped her up and refastened her bra. She noted his expertise and decided Tanner Jones was far more experienced than she, but then, most people were. Jimmy Jr. was her whole point of reference.

"Tell me again why we're waiting," Tanner said.

"So we can get to know each other first."

"Couldn't we sort of work on both things at once?"

She took his face in her hands. She longed to crush his mouth against hers once more, but she remembered her ultimate goal and resisted the urge. "You put your picture in *Texas Men* because you weren't happy with the relationships you'd had so far. Is that right?"

He sighed, as if knowing he'd lost the battle. "Yes, that's right."

"Besides throwing your money around, you probably rushed into intimacy with a woman, didn't you?"

"Maybe. But that was different, because—"

She laid her finger against his lips. "Not so different, perhaps. I won't let you ruin this. Not by spending too much money and not by making love before your heart's in it."

He leaned his forehead against hers and closed his eyes. "What if I told you my heart's in it now, right this minute, and the rest of me is dying to follow?"

"I'd say you're a sweet-talkin' man who's used to getting what he wants immediately. But you're here now, not in East Texas." She took a long, steadying breath. "And thanks to me you're going to learn the art of anticipation."

8

DORI DIDN'T THINK anything could affect her positive mood as she started her shift that afternoon at the Double Nickel. She smiled at Heck Tyrrell when she saw him sitting at the counter enjoying an order of liver and onions. "Didn't expect to see you again so soon, Heck."

"My rig's in the shop until three," he said after swallowing a bite of food. "Had to put up at the Prairie Schooner last night."

Dori thought about that while she took a couple of orders from people sitting in the booths and clipped them to the stainless-steel ticket carousel. Heck had more to say on the subject of staying at the Prairie Schooner. She could feel it. Well, she had nothing to hide or be ashamed of.

She picked up the coffeepot and moved down the counter, deliberately serving Heck last. "I stopped by the Prairie Schooner myself last night," she said casually.

"I know. Saw your car."

"I didn't stay long." Darn it, she sounded defensive when she had no reason to be.

Heck blew across the surface of his coffee and glanced up at her. "That's your business, how long you stayed."

Dori felt heat climb into her cheeks. "Heck—"

"Easy, Dori Mae. I'm not fixing to judge you. It ain't my place. Besides, I talked to that ol' boy later on. He ain't so bad considerin' he's from East Texas."

"You talked to him?" Dori wondered why Tanner had failed to mention that. "When?"

"When we had all the commotion out there. You didn't hear about it?"

"No. What—" She paused as the cook set an order on the pass-through and another customer took a seat at the counter. "Don't you move from that spot, Heck Tyrrell. I want to hear all about this commotion."

"I ain't goin' anywheres until three." Heck pushed away his empty plate and reached in his breast pocket for a toothpick.

A rush of business kept Dori busy for another fifteen minutes, but Heck sat patiently drinking coffee. Finally, she made it back to him, stuck her order pad and pencil in the pocket of her uniform and braced her elbows on the counter. "Now tell me about this commotion."

Heck took his toothpick from the corner of his mouth. "I figured you'd know about it by now. Some high school kids threw a stink bomb in one of the rooms. The parking lot smelled like a pig farm for quite a while. I guess the poor folks in the room had to borrow some clothes from Elmer and Beatrice while they washed every stitch they had."

"So that's when you talked to Tanner?"

"Yeah, everybody came out of their rooms to see what the ruckus was about. I recognized your new beau, so I decided to go over and say howdy. Check him out."

Dori noticed two truckers at the cash register, ready to pay. "Stay there," she instructed Heck. "I'll be right back."

A thought niggled at her as she finished the transaction for the truckers. She smiled at them as she closed the cash register. "Y'all come back now," she said automatically, but her thoughts were on the vandalism at the Prairie Schooner. It could be coincidence that the motel was hit soon after Tanner arrived there, but she didn't think so. Besides, Tanner hadn't mentioned the incident, maybe because he didn't want to worry her. That would be like Tanner, trying to protect her.

Finally, she poured coffee for everyone at the counter and topped off Heck's cup. "Are you sure it was high school kids?" she asked.

"Nothin' else makes sense. Those folks were from New Mexico, and they'd just stopped for one night. They didn't have time to get somebody riled enough to throw a stink bomb in their room in the middle of the night."

Dori lowered her voice. "Maybe it was meant for Tanner. Did you think of that?"

Heck glanced down the counter and leaned closer to Dori before he spoke. "Jimmy's information would've been better. He would've hit the right room."

"I suppose."

Soon after that Heck left and customers kept Dori busy for the next two hours. Yet she couldn't forget about the incident at the Prairie Schooner. The act was so like one Jimmy had pulled when he was a senior at Los Lobos High. The geometry teacher, Mr. Confer, had flunked him. He'd slit the screen of an open window of Mr. Confer's house and pitched a stink bomb inside. He hadn't been caught, but he couldn't resist bragging about it to Dori after they were married.

This time he'd probably have bribed a maid to find out Tanner's room number and then sent somebody else to throw the bomb. Jimmy wouldn't have risked being tied to the episode. And the only reason Tanner hadn't ended up with a stink bomb perfuming all his belongings was that Jimmy's hired punk had bombed the wrong room.

Or had he?

The Double Nickel had telephones in each of the booths for any truckers who wanted to call home. Dori looked up the number for the Prairie Schooner in the phone book the café kept behind the cash register. Then during a lull in business she slid into an empty booth and called the motel.

Elmer answered. "Dori! Did you and that ol' boy have a good time today?"

"We sure did, Elmer. Please thank Beatrice for the loan of her picnic basket. That was right generous of her."

"She thinks the world of you, Dori Mae, and we both feel bad about what you've been through. Your East Texan seems okay. Doesn't even act much like he's from the city."

"Well, he says you and Beatrice have been taking real good care of him, changing his room for him and all."

"Good thing we did, too! Some kids threw a stink bomb in the room he was in before."

Dori closed her eyes. So he hadn't been in room nine all along. He'd deliberately lied to her. It wasn't a big lie. Some would say it wasn't even worth bothering about. But she was putting her life, not to mention Little Jim's, on the line. With stakes like that, there was no such thing as a small lie.

TANNER HAD DECIDED to take Dori dancing after she got off work. Given his budget, he'd had to settle for the Golden Spur, a small bar on the outskirts of town. Elmer had told him to expect reasonable drink prices, a jukebox and a postage-stamp-sized dance floor. Elmer hadn't thought it would be very crowded on a Tuesday night.

When Tanner had picked Dori up at her house he'd been looking forward to the pleasures of a honky-tonk sort of evening, the kind he'd enjoyed years ago before he'd graduated to expensive nightclubs. He'd viewed Dori's choice of clothing with appreciation—a scoop-necked white blouse tucked into a colorful broomstick skirt. She'd looked feminine, sexy... and madder than a wet hen.

They'd ridden to the Golden Spur in silence, and now they sat across from each other at a small table right next to the tiny, deserted dance floor. A couple of cowboys sat at the bar a distance away from them, but otherwise the place was empty. Two draft beers sat sweating on two small napkins in front of Tanner and Dori. She hadn't touched hers.

Whatever was bothering her, she wasn't having much success broaching the subject. Tanner really hated to ask, because it seemed to be the equivalent of poking in a hollow tree with a stick to find out what the buzzing sound was all about. But finally he couldn't stand the tension any longer.

"Will you tell me about it?"

To his surprise her eyes filled with tears. She swiped at them with angry motions of both hands.

"Dori, for goodness' sake, what's wrong?"

She shoved away his hand as he reached for her. "I suppose you think it's real funny that somebody uses a lucky number to guide their actions."

"No, no I don't. I might not believe in it myself, but I respect—"

"The hell you do." Her voice was low and tight. "You used the information to hornswoggle me, though." She glared at him, unsuccessfully trying to hide her hurt behind a facade of anger. "Room nine. What a coincidence. And all the time you were laughing at me."

The bottom seemed to drop out of his stomach. The truth was his only defense. "I wasn't laughing. I thought I was going to lose you."

"So you made a mockery of my little superstition. How charming."

"No, I grabbed at the first thing I could think of to keep you around. Desperation makes people do all sorts of things." He captured her gaze with his and willed her to understand.

"Like lie?"

"I would have told you the truth about the room eventually. Sure, I manipulated the situation to my advantage, and I'd do it again, just to spend a morning like we shared, just to hold you in my arms one more time. I'll never forget the pleasure of touching you, Dori."

She glanced away, and color rose in her cheeks. "You're getting away from the subject."

"Am I? You told me yourself that you'd thought of sending me back to Dallas before you found out what room I had at the motel. I bought myself more time with you. I bought us more time."

Her eyes were large and shining with the vulnerability that had tugged at him when he'd first seen her picture. "And I suppose that makes it all right."

"For me it does. You'll have to answer for yourself."

She stared at him wordlessly, looking like a waxen image except for the gentle motion of her throat as she swallowed.

"Think about it for a minute," he said softly. "I'll be right back." He walked over to the silent jukebox and put coins in the slot. Then he picked out every damn song next to a number with a nine in it. He didn't even look at the selections. Maybe it was time to trust this mystical connection she had with a number. After all, it had gotten him this far. Maybe it would pull him out of this hole he was in.

He walked back to the table just as the opening chords of an Alan Jackson song surged from the jukebox. He gazed down at her. "Care to dance?"

She looked up at him, her heart in her eyes. Then slowly she stood and moved into his arms. He gathered her close with an unspoken prayer of gratitude. She wouldn't disappear from his life yet. Maybe in a few moments, when the song ended, she'd collect herself and order him to leave. But for now she wound one arm around his neck and laid her head on his shoulder. He held her hand cupped against his chest as they swayed, barely moving their feet.

Tanner rested his cheek against her silky hair and breathed in the fragrance as if he needed her scent to live. And maybe he did. Alan Jackson crooned about lovers being able to walk through fire without blinking, and Tanner understood completely. For the first time since he'd met Dori, his primary concern wasn't how soon he'd be able to make love to her. She could probably change his focus with a kiss, but for the moment he cherished the simple act of holding her. A desire for her body had been replaced by a desire for her trust.

He thought of all she didn't know about him and decided the time had come to tell her about his financial situation. Dori wasn't a gold digger. It wasn't in her nature to be greedy. But she valued the truth, and she deserved to have it. After this dance.

Gradually, she relaxed against him, and as the song ended she was snuggled so close, he hated to move and break the mood. The next song slipped into place on the jukebox, and it was another love ballad, this time by George Strait.

With a sigh Dori lifted her head and looked into Tanner's eyes as she swayed to the gentle rhythm. "I like your taste in songs."

"I didn't pick them."

"Of course you did. I watched you do it."

"I put in the money. Then I let your lucky number do the picking."

Her eyes narrowed. "Are you making fun of me again?"

"I never was making fun of you." He held her close and moved to the music. This subject wouldn't come between them again if he could help it. "And as you well know, changing to room nine saved me from that stink bomb. Without your belief in number nine, you wouldn't have bought the September issue of *Texas Men* or picked me out as the ninth bachelor. I owe that number a lot, so I decided to find out what happened if I abandoned myself to its power."

"You *are* making fun of me."

"Absolutely not." Her body was so warm, so supple, against his. "I'm more convinced than ever that you're on to something. You just said you liked the songs."

The suspicion gradually disappeared, leaving her eyes soft as a doe's. "They're so . . . romantic."

He caressed the small of her back. "And exactly what we needed."

"Promise to tell me the truth from now on, Tanner."

"I will," he vowed. *Right after this dance.* Sure, he could have led her back immediately to the table and resolutely presented the news of his healthy investment portfolio. Maybe there was a man somewhere with the strength to resist the petal-soft feel of her cheek against his, her gentle fragrance wafting from the tender spot behind her ear where women dabbed their cologne, her ripe woman's body undulating in time to the music. Tanner wasn't that man.

Somebody tapped him on the shoulder. He edged slowly out of his daze and turned, wondering if one of the idiots who'd been sitting at the bar really expected to cut in.

A young buck in a formfitting T-shirt that showed off his pecs stood behind Tanner. He adjusted his black Stetson. "You the ol' boy who owns that Chevy pickup out front?" he asked.

Technically, it belonged to one of his electricians. "Why?"

"Excuse me, ma'am." The cowboy tipped his hat toward Dori before facing Tanner again. "Your bucket of bolts just rolled into my truck, that's why, sucker. Don't they know about emergency brakes in East Texas?"

Tanner knew the guy was lying about the accident, if there even was one. He could be part of an insurance scam or he could be connected to Jimmy Jr. The East Texas crack indicated he knew who Tanner was, so Devaney could be behind it. Tanner would rather have it be about insurance. That would only take money to fix. He released Dori. "Why don't you go have some of that draft we ordered while I take care of this?"

She started to protest.

"Please."

She looked doubtful but made her way back to the table, where she glanced back at him, a worried expression on her face.

"Let's go take a look," Tanner said to the muscleman, whose sculpted body was probably more the result of constant contact with a weight machine than hours spent in honest labor.

The guy headed toward the front door of the bar. "Just got my truck painted, a primo job, too. I don't appreciate having some screwup like you ruin it just because he can't pull a damn handle."

Tanner remembered leaving the truck in gear, setting the emergency and locking both doors. But there was no alarm system, no security club for the wheel. Anybody with a slim-jim bar could have opened it, put it in neutral and released the brake.

Outside, the parking lot lights illuminated his electrician's old truck, the tailgate wedged against the dented passenger door of a cherry red pickup. It looked like a setup, but that wasn't what worried him. Three more bulked-up cowboys stood around the wreck, beer cans in hand, voices loud as they discussed the accident. When Tanner walked out they all looked up with a decidedly predatory expression.

"This the one?" asked a guy with a droopy mustache.

"Yeah," said the cowboy who had come into the bar. He swung back to Tanner. "See what you did to my truck? Somebody's gonna pay for that, and it sure as hell ain't gonna be me."

Tanner evaluated his chances against the four men. Not good. "I distinctly remember putting the car in gear and setting the brake," he said. "Besides that, I locked it."

"Did you now?" The truck owner sneered at him. "I don't think so, sucker. My friends here saw it all happen. We pulled in, figuring to grab us a beer at the Golden Spur, and just as we cruised by, your truck started rollin'. Couldn't get out of the way."

"You're lying, mister," Tanner said easily.

The truck owner glanced back at his pals. "You hear that? This ol' boy from East Texas called me a liar."

"Don't be lettin' him get away with that, Billy Joe."

There was an inevitable quality about the exchange. Tanner had pretty much known what to expect from the minute he walked out the door of the bar and saw the other guys. "We'll see what the insurance adjusters have to say about it," he said, reaching for his wallet to give the guy a card he didn't expect him to accept. This wasn't about vehicle repair.

"That usually takes a long time, don't it?" the truck owner said.

Tanner met his mocking gaze. "Depends on whether you have a legitimate claim."

"I don't think I want to wait for no insurance adjuster. I want satisfaction now."

"Too bad." Tanner watched the other three move closer. He flexed his shoulders and shifted his weight to the balls of his feet. "I don't carry much cash."

"Then I guess I'll have to take it out of your hide."

Tanner's knuckles smashed against the truck owner's jaw. It was the only punch he was able to throw before the others closed in.

DORI SIPPED HER BEER, but she kept a constant watch on the front door of the bar. Tanner's selections kept playing on the jukebox, and she loved all of them. She'd be sure and tell him as soon as he got back, which should be any minute. He and the cowboy would exchange insurance information and be done with it. She hoped Tanner carried good insurance. The way he was about money, he might have skimped on his coverage.

Interspersed with her thoughts was a remembered sound. She kept hearing the sound in her mind and wondered why. Finally, she identified it—the rasp of an emergency brake. She'd been preoccupied by her feelings of betrayal when they'd turned into the parking lot, and if the cowboy had asked her, she wouldn't have been able to swear whether Tanner had pulled on the brake. Except that he had. As she replayed their arrival in her mind, she heard him shut off the engine and set the brake.

She bolted from her chair and ran for the door. As she flung it open a red truck peeled out of the lot. Tanner lay crumpled on the ground.

With a cry she ran over and dropped to her knees beside him. His right eye was already swelling shut and he was bleeding from his nose. He looked blearily up at her with his one good eye. "Coulda taken him, 'cept for his three friends," he mumbled through a mouth cut and bleeding. Then he passed out.

9

THE NEXT COUPLE of hours were a scrambled nightmare for Dori. She instructed the bartender to call 9-1-1, which brought Deputy Holt in a squad car and Los Lobos's single licensed paramedic, Ned Fickett, in the volunteer fire department's truck. Tanner regained consciousness just as they arrived and protested all the attention for what he insisted were minor injuries. Nevertheless, the paramedic applied first aid and the deputy took a report. Dori wasn't able to identify the man who had entered the bar, and neither she nor Tanner could remember the license number of the truck.

On Ned Fickett's advice, Dori drove Tanner to the small emergency clinic for a more thorough examination. He was diagnosed with two cracked ribs, which were taped, a broken nose, which was splinted, and numerous gashes, which were bandaged. He wanted to drive when they left the clinic, but Dori refused to give him the keys to the truck.

When he allowed her to keep them, she knew how whipped he really was. She drove straight to her house, parked the truck defiantly in her driveway and helped him inside. She'd love Jimmy Jr. to make a big deal out of it. At this moment she felt that if he showed up she could do at least as much damage to him as his hired punks had done to Tanner. Every time Tanner winced, or she looked at the bruise darkening around his swollen eye, her rage grew.

With a supportive arm around his waist, she guided him down the hall toward her bedroom.

"Bad idea, coming here," he mumbled through swollen lips. "I can't promise I won't—"

"I can. You're a mess. And you're too big and too injured to cram yourself on the couch or Little Jim's bed. I'll sleep in my son's room tonight."

"Okay." He stumbled. "Sorry. Guess I'm a bit dizzy."

"No kidding." She pulled back the covers, sat him on the bed and started unbuttoning his shirt.

He allowed her to take that off, but when she reached for his belt buckle he caught her hand. "Don't test me," he muttered.

"You can do it?"

"You might be surprised what I can do." His smile ended in a groan as his split lip began bleeding again. "Got a washcloth?"

"Coming up." She hurried into the bathroom, dampened a red washcloth and brought it back. She dabbed at his lip.

"Can't see the blood," he said.

She glanced down at the washcloth. She'd automatically grabbed the one she used to clean up Little Jim's scratches. "On purpose. It keeps people from getting scared by seeing their own blood all over the place."

"Good idea." He sounded incredibly weary.

"The bleeding's stopped." She set the washcloth on the night table and helped him to his feet. "Let's get you into bed."

"Nicest offer I've had all night."

But she could tell, despite his lighthearted comments, that he felt as bad as he looked. "Are you sure you can get your jeans off by yourself?"

He nodded.

She stayed in the room just to make sure he didn't fall and hurt himself even worse. At least, she told herself that was the reason. He'd just been beaten up, for heaven's sake, so now wasn't an appropriate time to admire his strong-looking thighs or the substantial bulk contained in the crotch of his white briefs.

"You don't have to sleep in Little Jim's bed."

She glanced into his face with a guilty start. "Yes, I do. Goodness, Tanner, you have two cracked ribs. How can you even be thinking—"

"Weren't you?"

"I—" She could feel the blush spreading. "Never mind. Get under the covers. And I'll bet you could use a glass of water. And a fresh ice pack for your eye. I'll get them." She started toward the door.

"Sleep with me, Dori."

She paused, her back to him.

"We don't have to make love."

She shook her head.

"You don't trust me?"

"I trust you just fine. It's me I don't trust."

"Oh." Even through his weariness and pain, male satisfaction was obvious in that single syllable.

Dori left the room quickly.

By the time she returned with a soft-gel ice pack and a glass of water, Tanner had climbed into her bed and thrown a sheet over himself. His eyes were closed, and she thought he might have already gone to sleep. She crept to his bedside, set the glass of water down carefully and switched off the bedside lamp. Then she started to walk away.

"Don't go."

She turned back to him. "I thought you were asleep. Do you want the ice pack for your eye?"

"I'd rather have you lie down beside me."

"Tanner—"

"Outside the covers, if you want." He sighed. "I don't have any devious plans, unfortunately. I think the adrenaline rush is about gone, and I feel like hell."

"You need another pain pill." She reached for the bottle on the bedside table.

"I hate those damn things. They make me disoriented. Please, Dori. Just lie beside me. That's better than any painkiller they could prescribe."

"Okay." She walked around to the other side of the bed, took off her shoes and eased down on top of the bedspread, not wanting to jiggle him and cause him more discomfort. She laid her head on the pillow and gazed up at the shadowy ceiling above them.

In the darkness, his hand found hers and held it loosely as they lay together, their breathing the only sound in the room. Dori gradually relaxed as a floating, peaceful feeling traveled from their joined hands and spread throughout her tense body.

"The worst part of it was feeling so helpless," he said.

The peaceful feeling evaporated, and she didn't trust herself to speak. Thinking about him being beaten up by four men made her stomach churn.

"I haven't felt that much loss of control since I had my tonsils out when I was fifteen, and they put me under the anesthetic. I tried to fight back, but those guys operated like a trained machine."

She finally voiced a thought she'd had some time ago. "You knew it could turn out like that when you left the bar, didn't you?"

"I knew I'd set the brake. I was hoping it was all about insurance. Then I saw the three other guys and figured it wasn't."

Her jaw clenched. "Then why in heaven's name didn't you turn around and come back inside?"

"Because he just would have tried again later, with a new set of bullies. I decided to get this part over with."

"Oh, did you? And what's the next part, allowing him to have you killed?"

"He won't go that far."

She laughed in disbelief.

"No, seriously. This is just an old-fashioned brand of intimidation. Once he finds out that I'm still here, even after his boys beat me up, he'll search for a new tactic. I'm not sure what it'll be, but I think the physical part is over."

As Dori listened to him breathe, she thought of how every inhalation must hurt his cracked ribs. Yes, the physical intimidation was indeed over. She'd make sure of it. Beneath her rage at Jimmy and her impatience at Tanner's willingness to take such punishment lay a reservoir of guilt, boiling hot enough to scald her conscience. She'd brought Tanner into this situation. If she hadn't written to him, he wouldn't have a black eye, broken nose and cracked ribs. He'd be dating some other woman who had admired his picture in *Texas Men*. Some safe woman with a cozy apartment, and a cat, and no complications in her life.

Dori had to convince him to go back to Dallas, even if that meant giving up her idea of creating a two-parent household for Little Jim. Even if it meant giving up Tanner before she knew if they'd make wonderful lovers and best friends. No matter how much she wanted that, she wouldn't sacrifice another human being, let alone a dear man like Tanner, in her efforts to get it.

Maybe Jimmy Jr. wouldn't send another bunch of punks to use Tanner as a human punching bag, but then again maybe he would. It would be simple, really, to get Tanner out of town. She'd just tell him that she couldn't imagine a future together and he might as well go home and answer somebody else's letter. He couldn't argue with her if she told him she didn't want him.

She took a deep breath and shoved her own dreams and plans aside. Might as well get it over with. "Tanner?"

There was no response except for the sound of his breathing. She disengaged herself from his loose grip and propped herself up so she could study his face. He was asleep.

She tried to ignore a feeling of relief as she crept out of the bed and left the room. They'd still have to have their final conversation, of course. But not quite yet. She closed the door softly behind her and headed for her kitchen phone. It was nearly one in the morning, but she didn't give a damn. She had a call to make and the idea of waking up the Devaney household didn't faze her.

After five rings, James Devaney answered with a curt and impatient "Yes?"

"Let me speak to Jimmy."

"Dori, Jimmy Jr. is asleep." He sounded furious, but then he often sounded furious. "So is everyone else in this house, or, at least, we were. Are you drunk?"

"I am stone-cold sober, James." She'd seldom had the nerve to use his given name when she'd lived there. There was great satisfaction in using it tonight. "And I want to talk to your son. Now."

He raised his voice, one of his favorite tricks for sub-duing subordinates. "I'm hanging up this phone, Dori Mae. And don't you *ever* try to give me orders again."

"Did Jimmy tell you about throwing the stink bomb in Mr. Confer's window when he was a senior in high school?"

"What?"

"He told me. I imagine Deputy Holt would like to know about that little prank. The sheriff's department keeps records on things like that. He might be able to compare the type of bomb used with the type somebody tossed into a room at the Prairie Schooner Monday night."

"You *are* drunk, young lady. I—"

She heard the sound of him muffling the receiver.

Then the muffling disappeared. "Make it quick," James said from a distance. "I don't appreciate getting calls at one in the morning."

Jimmy Jr. came on the line. "Miss me, sweetheart? Want Jimmy to come over and make you feel good?"

"You arrogant, mean son of a bitch."

"Dori, honey, you know our women don't swear like that. It's so unbecomin' on somebody as pretty as you."

Her fingers tightened around the receiver. "You sent those punks to beat him up, didn't you?"

"I don't have the first clue what you're talkin' about, baby. Beat who up?"

"You did it, all right, just like you arranged to have the stink bomb thrown into his motel room. I know you, Jimmy. I'm telling Deputy Holt about the bomb you put in Mr. Confer's house. He was around then, probably remembers it real well. Maybe he can tie the two bombings together."

"I guess you got ahold of some locoweed, sweetheart. I didn't do any such thing as throw a stink bomb, either into old man Confer's house or the Prairie Schooner."

"You did! You told me exactly how!"

"But that'd be your word against mine, now wouldn't it? And everybody knows you're tryin' to get me in trouble, on account of Little Jim and all."

She ground her back teeth together. She'd thought that confession of his would give her some leverage, but he was right. It was his word against hers. She'd never mentioned the incident to any of her friends after Jimmy told her about it, not even after the divorce, because she'd imagined she owed Jimmy some loyalty considering she'd been the one who'd left the marriage. She should have taken out an ad in the Los Lobos *Weekly Tribune* listing all Jimmy Jr.'s transgressions.

"Little Jim asked me again when you were coming home, Dori Mae."

"You know something, Jimmy? Last Sunday I thought I might be able to put up with you if that was my last resort for getting to be with Little Jim every day. But the way you've acted with Tanner, I know I couldn't humiliate myself that much, even for Little Jim. Get this straight. I'm never coming back. Never." She slammed down the phone—a small victory and cold comfort, considering that she wasn't in a very wonderful position right now. But the gesture felt good, nonetheless.

It was very late, and she'd been through a lot today, she thought, yawning. She made sure the house was secure, flipped out the lights in the kitchen and living room and went to check on Tanner. He slept, looking vulnerable with his splint on his nose and his taped chest visible where the sheet had pulled back. She placed a kiss on the tips of her fingers and touched his cheek lightly. He moaned and shifted to his side, but didn't awaken.

"Sleep well, my hero," she whispered. "You've been wonderful, and far more than I deserve."

Then she went into Little Jim's room. Her night things were back in her bedroom, so she decided to sleep in her panties and her white blouse rather than risk disturbing Tanner. Pulling back the spread, she slipped into his narrow twin bed, made even narrower by all the stuffed animals grouped on it.

She lay in the darkness, expecting sleep. But only grief arrived. She'd tried so hard to remedy the mistake she'd made when she'd said "I do" to Jimmy Jr. Nothing seemed to be working, and she'd brought misery to a good man in the process of searching for a solution. She pulled Little Jim's favorite bear close and its soft fur absorbed her tears.

WHEN TANNER FIRST TRIED to open his eyes, he thought he must have the hangover of the decade. Then gradually he remembered the night before and the four weight lifters dressed like cowboys. He'd be willing to bet they'd been imported from Amarillo, or even as far away as El Paso. The cherry red truck was probably in some chopshop by now, being dismantled for parts so no evidence would remain.

And he was in Dori's bed, surrounded by a million pictures of her son. She'd left him sometime during the night, probably to snuggle in with Little Jim's collection of furry friends. He raised himself up slowly, and discovered his head wasn't spinning the way it had last night. Sure, he hurt, but at least he was awake. Last night he'd been spaced out on the damn painkillers, and God knows what he'd said. Probably acted like a complete idiot.

He pulled on his jeans, took the bottle of pills from the bedside table on his way to the bathroom and flushed them away. Enough of that nonsense. He took a quick look at himself in the mirror and almost wished he hadn't. Now there was a face to inspire love in a fair damsel. Maybe if she was into the legend of Beauty and the Beast, he'd have a better than even chance.

Debating the issue for only a moment, he used the spare toothbrush she'd put out for him and the razor she kept in the shower for her legs. A guy who looked like the Phantom of the Opera needed all the help he could get.

The house was quiet as he walked barefoot down the hall. Sure enough, she was in Little Jim's twin bed, at least four stuffed animals gathered into her arms as she slept. In his estimation she needed something more substantial to hold, something with a pulse. And this morning, thanks to the healing powers of sleep, he had one.

Her kitchen was easy to figure out. She'd put things where he would have if he'd been deciding. That was probably a good sign, and he should remember to tell her about it later. Breakfast was the only meal of the day he normally fixed for himself, and he set about brewing coffee and pouring juice with a practiced hand. With each step he marveled that she had the exact supplies he would have required in his own place.

Today he'd tell her about his high-rise luxury apartment unit in Dallas, his Jaguar in the apartment's underground garage, his small cabin in the lake country and his yacht moored in Galveston Harbor. He'd explain how he'd caught the boom in the bedroom community of Bravo, east of Dallas, where homes sold for millions and builders with vision could name their price. He'd been that sort of builder.

He soft-boiled a couple of eggs, toasted some whole-wheat bread and was ready to bring her breakfast on a tray. It seemed like the perfect gesture after she'd cared for him so capably the night before. Apparently, she'd driven the truck without a flicker of doubt, and brought him home with her rather than dump him at an impersonal motel. That was also a good sign. He'd build on that.

A selection of trays sat on top of the refrigerator, and he found one in wicker that held everything he'd created. On an impulse, he went out the front door to pick a chrysanthemum for the tray. There in the driveway sat his electrician's truck, the side spray-painted in white with the message Go Home, City Boy. Sweet. His electrician, Jay, would end up with a paint job on his truck as well as a tailgate and rear bumper replacement.

If this was Jimmy Jr.'s next move, it lacked originality. Tanner could live with a little spray paint. He picked his chrysanthemum, a striking orange one, and stuck it in the bud vase he'd found in a cabinet over the stove. Closing the front door, he latched the dead bolt and picked up the tray, complete with flower. Time for his lady fair to awaken.

He set the tray on the brightly painted child's dresser against the wall near the bed. The tray shared the surface with the White Ranger. Then he crouched down so his face was even with Dori's. For a moment he watched her sleep, her rosy lips slightly parted, her wondrous eyes shuttered, her luxuriant eyelashes resting against her cheeks. His heart contracted. This view could be his every morning. The possibility made his throat ache with longing.

Leaning closer, he angled his mouth and brushed a kiss against her sleep-softened lips. He barely noticed the slight sting of discomfort from his split lip, because he was so entranced by her response. She turned her face upward, as if seeking the source of pleasure as she struggled toward wakefulness. Needing no more encouragement, he placed his mouth over hers again and stroked his tongue inside. Yes. He wanted this every morning.

She wound her arms around his neck and drew him down. He pushed the stuffed animals out of the way, threw back the light cover and eased over her. He would have loved to have more room, but if she was inviting him to bed he wouldn't be choosy about the details. As he settled against her breasts he winced at the pain from his taped ribs, but he was more impatient with the tape than the pain. It kept him from a total experience of skin touching skin.

Because that would happen now. She would let him love her. She was too warm, too willing, for there to be any other outcome.

As he continued to plunder her lips, he reached between them to pull the end of the tie that gathered her blouse into a modest scooped neck. Once the tie was released, the neckline became much less modest, giving him easy access to her breasts. Filling one hand with her bounty, he released her mouth and raised his head. He wanted to see her eyes.

Slowly, they fluttered open. The passion filling their brown depths made his heart pound.

"Good morning," he murmured as he caressed her, his thumb brushing over her nipple. "I brought you breakfast in bed."

Her voice was husky from sleep and desire. "Is this it?"

"Chef's special."

"I was going to ask you to leave town this morning."

"Oh?" He cupped her other breast and continued to build the heat in her gaze.

She arched against his hand with a soft moan. "You're not safe here."

He grazed her nipple with his thumb until it matched the pert attention of its mate. "And what made you think I'd agree to go?"

"I was . . ." She paused, caught her lower lip between her teeth and closed her eyes. "Oh, Tanner," she whispered. "That feels so good."

"Want me to leave town?"

"No. Yes." She opened her eyes again, rich laughter mixing with the desire in her glance. "But you're ruining the line I'd planned to use."

"Which was?"

"That I didn't want you."

He smiled down at her. "I wouldn't have believed you, anyway." He released her breast and worked the blouse off her shoulders. "You may not like the way I spend money, but you've always been crazy about the way I kiss you."

Her voice was low and sexy. "Conceited man."

"Lucky man." He kissed the pulse throbbing in her throat and breathed in the scent of wildflowers and arousal. "You're going to let me make love to you this morning."

"Am I?"

"Yes." He lifted his head to look into her eyes.

"No," she murmured, a sensuous smile curving her mouth.

"You're kidding." He ached all over from wanting her. A woman who could deny a man at this stage . . .

"I'm not kidding. You're not going to make love to me. You're injured."

"I don't give a good goddamn! I want—"

"So I'll make love to you."

He stared down at her.

"In a bigger bed. So we have room to enjoy this. Come on, Tanner. Move it."

10

TANNER HAD EXPECTED Dori to be alluring, voluptuous and deeply satisfying. He hadn't expected her to be an artist. He'd known that her mouth tempted him beyond reason. He'd hadn't known her mouth could carry him to levels of excitement he'd never experienced.

He lay trembling beneath the sweet assault, which began with his lips. Her kiss was so openly provocative he could hardly believe this was the same Dori Mae who had primly tucked her shirt back in her jeans at the motel on Monday night. She used her tongue to outline his lips, to explore the roof of his mouth, to stroke the inside of his cheeks. Then she drew his tongue into her mouth and sucked gently, giving him his first preview of what she had in mind. Her kiss alone brought him to a fever pitch of need, but she'd only begun.

She caught his earlobe between her teeth and raked gently. He'd never known he was so sensitive there, but that was nothing compared to the sensation she created by dipping her tongue into his ear. As she licked the curve of his jaw and the hollow of his throat, the warm, damp caress ignited nerve endings he hadn't known existed.

Then her sweet breath touched his shoulder, and she nibbled her way down his inner arm to the inside of his elbow. He'd been told women liked to be kissed there. Now he knew why.

Her journey continued to the palm of his hand, where she ran her tongue into the crevices between his fingers before taking each finger in turn into her mouth. He was a wild man, desperate for release yet never wanting the experience to end. She toyed with his nipples until he was panting, but she never put any weight on his taped ribs. When her tongue found his navel, he moaned in anticipation, but she had more sweet torture in mind before giving him her final gift.

She treated his toes to the same attention she had his fingers, and gently bent his legs to kiss the backs of his knees. The warmth of her mouth on his inner thighs nearly destroyed him. She licked higher, and he held his breath. The woman had a real sense of drama.

When she finally enclosed him with her clever mouth, he let out a shameless groan of pleasure. In moments, she had him deliriously close to losing control, which he'd promised himself not to do. He'd always prided himself on being able to hold a climax at bay, but this . . . Finally, in desperation, he asked her to stop.

She did, moving upward to gaze into his eyes. "You didn't like it?"

"I loved every incredible moment. Too much. I'm not leaving you behind."

Her smile was the first shy thing he'd seen about her since they entered her bedroom. "I wouldn't mind. You really are injured, and I—"

"I would mind." He reached up to cup her cheek. "This is about mutual pleasure, and I'm not so crippled that I can't do my part."

Her expression was hopeful, but hesitant. "Tanner, I'm not very . . . I have trouble . . ."

He almost swore, but he swallowed the first word that came to him. It didn't belong in a room where such incredible lovemaking was going on. That ass Devaney had taught her how to please, but not how to be pleased. He pulled her down for a long, slow kiss. Then he rolled to his side, bringing her with him. The pain didn't matter. She deserved this.

"Leave everything to me," he murmured, reaching behind him for the packet he'd tossed on the bedside table. He didn't want to stop in the middle of loving her to put on a condom. A woman as nervous about her response as Dori could lose everything he'd worked to build in the seconds it took him to sheath himself.

When he finished the job she was gazing at him. "I don't want you to worry about me," she said. "I know men can't always control when they. . . I mean, they're so much faster, and I . . . I'll . . . be fine, Tanner. Truly."

He gave her a lopsided smile. "Yes, ma'am, you'll be mighty fine."

"I—"

"Hush." Then he guaranteed that she'd drop the subject by leaning over her and kissing her until her breath grew fast and shallow. That quickened breath made kissing her breasts all the more exciting as she quivered beneath him. He took his time. She needed to be at the brink, perhaps beyond. It might require mere days to undo the damage her selfish ex-husband had done; it might take years. He hoped with all his heart he'd be hired for the job.

He allowed instinct to guide him. He kept his mouth at her breast as he caressed her flat belly and slid his hand down, combing his fingers through her silken curls. His first touch was light, questing. She tensed, as if expecting rougher treatment to follow. He silently cursed his predecessor one more time and teased her gently once again, and again, until she began to relax.

Her ascent was gradual but steady as he coaxed her along and slowly increased the pressure of his stroking fingers. He wanted to shout with joy when she began to lead, opening her thighs and lifting her hips for his caress. Her panting became inarticulate cries of passion. Close now. He lifted his mouth from her breast and shifted his position while he maintained a constant rhythm, bringing her closer still.

He continued stroking her as he moved between her thighs. He was nearly bursting himself, but he had to hold back, no matter how much he wanted to lose himself in her. Gradually, he replaced the touch of his hand with the slow slide of his penis. She gasped and brought her hips up to meet him.

He looked deep into her eyes as he pushed forward, withdrew and pushed forward again.

Her eyes widened and she clutched his shoulders. "Tanner," she whispered.

"Let go." He felt her first tremor and increased the rhythm. "That's it."

"I . . . oh!" Her lips parted as she drank in air, and then her world exploded.

The violent contractions destroyed his resolution to let her enjoy herself without his pleasure interfering. The torrent rushed from him with such force he cried out, submerged in an intensity that left him breathless and disoriented. Gradually, through the whirling in his head, came the sound of her voice murmuring. He listened, and realized she was reciting his name, over and over. He'd never heard it said quite that way, with a combination of awe and possessive delight. At that moment he knew he would give everything he owned to hear her say his name like that for the rest of his life.

DORI INSISTED ON EATING the cold eggs and toast, although she allowed Tanner to make a fresh cup of coffee. "Wasting food is another bad habit," she chided him, although her heart wasn't in it. They sat at her oak kitchen table, she in her housecoat and Tanner in his jeans. It had happened, the thing she'd most feared. She was too entranced with Tanner's lovemaking to give a fig about whether he was financially responsible or not.

She reached out her foot and caressed his bare toes under the table. "Well, you may be a little loose with money," she said, "but at least you're not rich." She was surprised at his reaction, almost as if she'd slapped him. "What did I say?"

He took a sip of his coffee before glancing up at her again. "I've just never had a woman mention it was great that I didn't have any money. I thought women always preferred a guy with a good income."

"A good income is okay. A good income would be very nice, as a matter of fact. I was talking about filthy rich, like the Devaneys. And in their case, *filthy* is the right word."

"I'm no lover of the Devaneys, especially the sleaze-ball Devaney you were married to, but I don't think their behavior has anything to do with money. I think they'd be rotten rich or poor."

"Maybe." Dori got up to get the coffee carafe and re-fill their cups.

"I could have done that," he said with a gentle smile.

"Habit," she said, topping off his cup. "You can take the waitress out of the café but you can't take the café out of the waitress."

Tanner leaned back in his chair to study her. "Are you happy with your job?"

"Everything except the pay," she said with a chuckle. Then she replaced the carafe and shut off the heat, buy-ing herself some thinking time before she returned to the table. His question set off a warning in her brain. "To be honest, I don't mind waitressing. It's good, honest work, and I'm performing a service those truckers desperately need."

"Feeding them and pouring coffee?"

Her uneasiness grew. "That, of course, but mostly the conversation." She sat at the table and curved her hand around her coffee mug. "People that move around as much as truck drivers need some things to be predict-able. They seem to appreciate coming into the Double Nickel and knowing they'll be able to talk to me, same as they did last time they stopped in. It makes them feel more secure, somehow."

Tanner nodded. "That makes sense."

She decided to turn the question back on him. "How about you? Would you rather be doing something else besides construction?"

"Not really. I love watching a house take shape, knowing that people will have a solid, beautiful place to come home to, a refuge from the rat race."

Dori laughed. "Then you must have some trouble when you're working on an office building."

"Actually, I don't work on them anymore. Just houses."

"Because you like them better?"

"Yep."

She took a sip of her coffee. So, he was picky about the jobs he accepted. Not a good sign. "In this economy I wouldn't think you could afford to be that choosy."

"Dori, I'm better off financially than you think. In fact, I—"

"Wait." She held up one hand. "I've been afraid where this discussion was leading to the moment you asked if I was happy with my job. We've had a lovely morning, Tanner. Please don't spoil it by telling me that you wouldn't want me to work if we get married. Because I always plan to work. Partly because I like it, and partly to maintain a balance of power."

He sat forward, a look of astonishment on his face. "Excuse me?"

"Money is power. I learned that the hard way with Jimmy Jr. Keeping my job seemed silly after we got married. And even if I had, my piddly little income wouldn't have been enough to balance against all the money Jimmy had."

Tanner leaned toward her. "But if two people love each other, then who has the money shouldn't matter."

"Ha. That's what I thought at eighteen. At twenty-seven I know better. It's the Golden Rule. The one who has the gold makes the rules." She waved a hand out the window. "Look around you. It works in business, and it works in marriage, too. I would never marry a rich man again, or quit work and depend entirely on my husband's income. It's not worth a hundred trips to Hawaii to have someone lord it over me financially."

"But—"

"That's it, Tanner. I want economic equality in my next marriage. End of discussion."

Tanner gazed at her, a thoughtful expression on his face. "I see."

"You *were* going to ask me about giving up my job, weren't you?"

His tone was guarded. "Not exactly. But I'm glad you told me how you feel. I'm not sure I agree with you about the money-and-power thing, but it's good to know up front what you're thinking is on the subject."

Dori didn't care for his answer. Although he didn't come right out and say so, he could very well have some ideas about women that clashed with hers. "Tanner, are you one of those men who deep down believes a woman's place is in the home?"

"I—no. No, I don't. My sister is studying law, after all."

"But your mother didn't work outside the home, did she?"

He hesitated. "No."

"Who makes the financial decisions in that marriage?"

He looked uncomfortable. "My father."

"You see, this is why I didn't want to make love too soon. We should have had this discussion before we—"

"No, you don't." He was out of his chair and pulling her from hers before she knew what was happening. "Don't be putting guilt on either of us for this morning.

You didn't want me to spoil it by asking you to be a stay-at-home wife." He wrapped his arms around her and brought her in close. "Don't you spoil it by saying it was a mistake we'll both regret."

"But my goal was not to let sexual attraction muddle my thinking." She felt his arousal through the terry cloth of her housecoat, and immediately she responded with a rush of moisture.

He rubbed his hands over her bottom in a sensuous kneading motion. "And is that happening?"

"Yes, that's happening, and I don't think—"

"Then I must be doing something right." Capturing her mouth, he slid both hands inside her housecoat.

She was helpless once he did that. The memory of the pleasure he'd given her earlier fueled what was already strong chemistry. Yesterday she'd wanted him without knowing what making love to him could mean. Now she knew, and the thought of repeating the experience drove her crazy with anticipation.

When he backed her down the hall to her bedroom, his hands and mouth already preparing her for what was to come, she didn't protest. By the time they got through the door she had opened the front of his jeans to run her hands over the instrument of her satisfaction. In seconds they'd shed their clothes and he'd rolled a condom over his erection.

But when he lay on his back and started to guide her on top of him, she felt a wave of disappointment.

He caught her face in her hands. "What is it?"

"Nothing." She leaned down and kissed him. "Nothing at all."

He held her slightly away from him. "Dori, I saw that look in your eyes, as if somebody had snatched away your favorite Christmas present and thrown it into the fireplace."

Heat seared her face. "Last time was so . . . lovely. But if we make love this way, I . . ." She didn't have the courage to go on.

"Yes, you will," he promised, looking into her eyes. "I haven't let you down yet."

"No, you sure haven't, Tanner."

He bracketed her hips with his hands. "Come here, sexy lady."

She straddled his hips, and he guided her slowly, sensuously down over his waiting shaft.

He sucked in a breath. "You are so fine, Dori." He cradled her breasts. "Lean down and let me taste you."

She braced her hands on either side of his head and lowered her breasts to his mouth. As he suckled, the tightening began again deep within her, the tightening that had led to such wonder not long ago. Almost instinctively she initiated a gentle rhythm that allowed his mouth to continue to tantalize her nipple. She began to throb with a remembered pulse. Ahh.

The tension built, and he let her guide their progress. She moaned softly, reaching for that tumbling free-fall that was like no other feeling on earth. As if sensing her eagerness, he slipped his hand up her thigh and pressed his thumb deep to the wellspring of her response. Her own movement provided the delicious friction that drove her closer to the precipice. The speed was in her control, and it was a dizzying experience.

Instead of racing headlong to her satisfaction, she felt it coming and held back. She savored it, then moved closer, and again retreated to prolong the inevitable. Tanner never coaxed, never projected his own needs. When she'd toyed with ecstasy beyond endurance, she gave herself the final reward, shuddering with a cataclysmic, joyful feeling of release.

Only then did his mouth leave her breast as he grasped her hips and urged her to a new motion. "Now, Dori," he murmured. "Now, sweetheart. Ahh, yes. Ahh, so good. There. Like that." His moan of surrender as he surged upward, lost in the moment, filled her with joy.

She rested her head in the curve of his shoulder while her breathing gradually slowed. She'd never known anything like the excitement they could generate together. It left her dazed with its potency and greedy for more. Their personal philosophies might be different, she thought as they lay sated and slicked with moisture, but only a foolish woman would turn away from a man who could love like this.

DORI SUGGESTED that Tanner check out of the Prairie Schooner and move his things to her house. He was willing to keep the room if she was worried about appearances, but she seemed more interested in the time they could spend in each other's company than appearances. That was a gigantic step in a community as tight as Los Lobos, and Tanner didn't minimize the extent of her commitment when she suggested the move.

She'd become furious when she looked out the front door for the first time and noticed the spray-painted truck. Tanner had shrugged it off to keep her from flying off the handle and doing something that could jeopardize her or her son. Once she was safely on her way to work, Tanner fired up the truck's engine and headed toward Devaney Trucking.

The outer office of the low building housing the trucking company was neat but unimposing. Imitation pine-paneled wallboard, gray indoor-outdoor carpeting and steel office furniture indicated an interest in utility rather than decor. A young blonde who looked like a recent prom queen sat at the desk that had the "receptionist" nameplate positioned at its front edge.

She blinked in apparent concern when Tanner walked in. "Goodness, have you been in an accident?" she asked, obviously forgetting the standard "Can I help you" drill.

"You might say that." He glanced down a hallway that began about five feet behind her desk. That was his destination. "I'd like to see Jimmy Devaney, Jr."

"If it's about a job, you'll have to fill out an application first." She rose and turned toward the bank of file cabinets, revealing a very short skirt and spectacular legs.

"I don't want a job."

"Oh." She turned back to him. "Do you have an appointment?"

"No. Is he here?"

Her sympathy for his battered face was replaced with a professional mask. "I'm afraid I'll need more information. May I have your name and the purpose of your visit?"

Tanner figured if he gave his name and she buzzed the Devaney heir with the information, the cowardly son of a bitch would take a back way out of the building and

Tanner would be left standing in the outer office like a jilted bridegroom. The image didn't please him.

"It's a surprise," he said with the most engaging grin he could manage considering his split lip and black eye. "I'll just go and find that ol' boy."

The blonde moved as if to stop him. "I don't think that's a good idea, Mr.—"

"Trust me." He strode past her with the bluffing technique that had seen him through several financial crises on his way to the top. "It's a fine idea."

She trailed behind him as he walked down the hall. He expected that Jimmy Jr. would have the first office and his father the one in the back, with more potential for space and prestige. He was right. The door immediately on his left had Jimmy's name stenciled on it. Tanner seized the knob, turned it and walked in. He shut the door in the receptionist's face and twisted the lock.

"What the hell?" Devaney looked up from the magazine he was reading. It looked like an issue of *Playboy*.

Tanner moved while the element of surprise was still in his favor. He rounded the desk and pulled Devaney up by his shirtfront. The man looked scared spitless, which was exactly how Tanner wanted him.

"Didn't expect to see me again, did you?" he rasped as Devaney gulped like a beached trout. "Get this straight, punk. You make a move against me again and I'll wait for you. You'll never know when it'll come, but it'll come, and I won't need three other guys to put you away." He shoved Devaney back in the chair.

As he walked toward the door, Devaney found his voice. "You can't talk to me like that!"

Tanner flipped open the lock on the door and turned back to Dori's ex-husband. "I just did." Then he left the office and smiled at the pretty receptionist on the way out.

11

TANNER DROVE from Devaney Trucking to the Prairie Schooner Motel to pick up his clothes and settle his bill.

"No charge," Elmer said when Tanner walked into the motel office and dug out his wallet.

Tanner stopped in mid-motion and looked at the gray-haired man in surprise. "I can pay," he said. "I know the truck looks old, but I—"

"Doesn't matter if you're King Midas hisself." Elmer peered at Tanner through thick bifocals. "Beatrice would have my hide if I was to charge you anything, considerin' all you've been through since you hit town."

Tanner nodded. "It's been interesting, all right." He paused. "You know you've got a security leak at the motel. That stink bomb was meant for me."

"I know it. We can't pay the maids much, y'know, and I'm pretty sure which one of them took the money to tell what room you was in. I'm watchin' her real close."

"Did that couple from New Mexico ever get the smell out of their clothes?"

"Yeah, with some help from Beatrice. Refunded their room rent, o' course. Lucky for us they didn't decide to sue."

"It hasn't been a very profitable few days, has it?"

Elmer shrugged. "You know how it is. We all manage to get by somehow."

"Well, thank you for the nice gesture." Tanner reached across the counter and offered his hand to Elmer. "I'm sure Dori appreciates it, too." Tanner knew better than to insist on paying, but he felt guilty all the same. He could afford the rent a lot more than Elmer and Beatrice could afford to lose it.

"You tell Dori Mae we're rootin' for y'all," Elmer said. "And I'll give you a tip, son. Marry the girl as quick as you can. People in these parts don't cotton to others livin' together without being joined in holy matrimony."

"Good," Tanner said. "Maybe that will hurry the lady along to a decision." He touched the brim of his Stetson, picked up his duffel bag and left the motel office.

On the drive to Dori's house he couldn't help wondering if Elmer would have been so friendly if he'd known Tanner could buy and sell him. Probably not. But Elmer wasn't the person Tanner was most concerned about. Dori's statement played over and over in his mind. *I would never marry a rich man again.*

Maybe it served him right. He'd been so determined to find a woman who wasn't lured by wealth that he'd found one who was repelled by it. And the joke was on him, because this was the woman he had to have. He craved everything about her—her unbreakable spirit, her devotion to her child, her generosity and her largely untapped passion. He'd fallen irrevocably, completely and happily in love.

He stopped by the local Piggly Wiggly on his way back to Dori's house and picked up a few things for a late-evening snack, keeping her budget for him in mind. He'd decided to postpone any announcement of his financial status for the time being. Their connection was too new and fragile to withstand that sort of information, given her deep-rooted prejudice.

And prejudice it was, though an understandable one. His willingness to let her lead in bed after she'd proclaimed her need for independence had been a subtle message. He'd deliver more of them before he told her the complete truth about himself. Funny, but his goal hadn't really changed. He still had to convince a woman to love him for himself and ignore what he possessed.

He reached her house and let himself in with the spare key she'd given him. Then he set about organizing romance on a shoestring. When she came home he wanted her to be transported to a world where there were no jealous ex-husbands, no difficult customers, no disappointing tips.

He carried her small oak table into the living room and located a white tablecloth tucked in the linen closet. The single candle had been on sale, but he hadn't thought what to put it in. Then he remembered the six-pack of long-necks he'd bought, thinking he'd like to have some beer around for the rest of the week. He'd just drink one and use the bottle for a candle holder.

Pulling the bottle from Dori's little refrigerator, he uncapped it and took a drink. He couldn't believe how much fun he was having planning a cheap evening at home. He'd become accustomed to dropping big sums of money when he entertained women, and he'd unconsciously fallen into the trap of thinking you could measure the kind of time you had by how much you spent.

He leaned one hip against her sink and glanced out the kitchen window toward the Devaney mansion. Tanner would describe it as the Devaney monstrosity. Whoever had designed that gigantic block of rooms should be shot. Dori's little house had more charm, because it was an honest, utilitarian dwelling that didn't pretend to be something it wasn't.

His shirt chafed against the tape around his ribs, and he unbuttoned it, leaving it hanging open as he turned away from the uninspiring view out the kitchen window. He and Dori would get Little Jim out of that stifling atmosphere, no matter how much time and money it took.

When the doorbell chimed, Tanner feared a delegation of churchgoers had arrived to protest his and Dori's living arrangements. He wouldn't have been terribly surprised. The people around here took their morals very seriously, as evidenced by Elmer's remark. He set the beer on the counter and walked to the front door.

He opened it to find Little Jim gazing up at him in total shock. Tanner remembered his bandaged nose and black eye. Little Jim was holding the hand of a very attractive blonde who looked barely forty and obviously understood dressing to attract male admiration. Her beige dress dipped softly and subtly to reveal cleavage and wrapped her hips to accentuate her womanly curves. The whole thing looked as if it would come off with the removal of one strategically placed decorative pin.

"Tanner, what *happened?*" Little Jim asked.

"Just clumsy," Tanner said. "Ran into a door."

"You look terrible."

Tanner smiled. "Thanks."

The woman stepped forward. "I'm Crystal Devaney, Little Jim's grandmother," she said. "May we come in?"

He knew modern grandmothers didn't look like the Norman Rockwell version anymore, but still he was taken aback. He revised his estimate of her age upward by about ten years. "Sure. Come in." He stepped back and let them pass.

"L.J., go play in your room while Mr. Jones and I talk," she ordered.

Little Jim's glance was hopeful as he directed it toward Tanner. "Is the White Ranger in my room?"

"Last time I checked."

"Oh, boy!" He tore off in search of his treasure.

Tanner watched him go. Then he turned back to Crystal and found her staring at his bandaged chest. "Uh, sorry, ma'am." He started buttoning his shirt.

She fingered the clasp on her elegantly miniaturized shoulder purse. "You've been in some terrible sort of fight, haven't you?"

He gave her a level look. "You could say that."

"I have a dreadful feeling it had something to do with my son. He dotes on that girl, you know."

"Mmm."

She glanced around the room. "Could we . . . sit down or something?"

He supposed he should be at least marginally polite, although he doubted Dori would want him to roll out the red carpet. Still, he was very curious as to what had prompted Crystal Devaney to show up in her powder blue Cadillac coupe. He waved her toward the couch. "By all means. I was having a beer. Would you like one?"

"That would be very nice."

When Tanner returned with his half-empty bottle and Crystal's beer in a glass he'd unearthed, he could hear the sound of an imaginary space battle going on in Little Jim's room. Probably the White Ranger against an invasion of aliens disguised as teddy bears. He handed Crystal the glass and a napkin before sitting on the opposite end of the couch. She set her purse next to her and crossed her legs. The skirt of her dress inched up, probably on purpose, to reveal excellently toned calves and thighs. This was a woman used to using her appearance to get what she wanted, he thought. Good thing she had no idea she was dealing with a corporate executive who'd seen all those moves before.

"Thank you kindly." She took a dainty sip. "Elmer told me you'd checked out today, and although he didn't say where you were, I guessed you might be here. So I took the liberty of calling on you."

"You probably knew it was the right place when you saw the spray painting on the side of my truck."

Her green eyes, the genetic predecessor of Jimmy Jr.'s and Little Jim's, clouded in apparent distress. "I hate all this ugliness. I truly do. I'd like to put a stop to it."

"That would be terrific."

"But I need your help, Mr. Jones."

Uh-oh. Here it comes. "Is that right?"

She lowered her voice and leaned forward, as if to make them coconspirators. Her cleavage became more visible. "It's for L.J. that I'm askin', Mr. Jones. That little boy needs his momma and daddy livin' in the same house again. They've had a lovers' spat, that's all. Nothing that a second honeymoon in the Caribbean wouldn't cure."

Something deep in Tanner rebelled. He'd already become possessive enough not to want Dori in any other man's arms, but the specific idea of her sharing a marriage bed again with Jimmy Devaney, Jr., made him a little crazy. "If I understand Dori correctly, and I think I'm in a position to do that, she'd rather roll a walnut with her nose five miles down the main street of Los Lobos, immediately following the Los Lobos sheriff's mounted posse, than have anything more to do with your son."

Crystal's hoot of laughter surprised him. "I didn't expect you to be so clever." She batted her eyelashes. "I'm beginning to see why Dori is so distracted by you."

"She's not distracted, Mrs. Devaney. She knows exactly what she wants."

"Please call me Crystal. Everyone does."

"Grandma, can I come out now?" Little Jim stood in the hallway clutching his White Ranger.

"Except this little devil," Crystal amended. "Come here, L.J."

Little Jim walked over to the couch and stood by her knee.

"What's the one thing you want more than anything in the world?" she asked him.

"All the Power Ranger stuff."

Crystal rolled her eyes. "No. What do you *really* want?"

Little Jim took a deep breath, as if about to recite. "Momma and Daddy back together." It was almost a chant.

Crystal glanced at Tanner, her eyebrows raised as if to say, "See there?"

Tanner was sickened. Encouraging the kid to believe in a happily-ever-after for his parents, who'd never belonged together in the first place, was just plain cruel.

"Hey, Jim," he said. "I think there's some orange soda in the refrigerator. And that swing set out back looks as if nobody's played on it in a long time. Why don't you get the soda and show the White Ranger all your secret places in the backyard?"

The boy's eyes widened. "How did you know I had secret places?"

Tanner smiled at him. "Good guess."

Little Jim gave him an admiring glance before he headed into the kitchen.

Once Tanner heard the back door close, he turned to Crystal. "Face reality, Crystal. Dori doesn't want to be married to your son. Accept that and stop making life more miserable for that little boy by pretending there will be a reconciliation. There won't."

"You can't know that!"

He held her gaze. "Oh, yes, I can."

"You're the problem." She stared into her glass of beer. Her lower lip had begun to quiver as her composure slipped. "I know they won't get together as long as you're around. She imagines you as some white knight dashing into town to make everything all right. What a foolish thought."

"Only if you don't believe in white knights."

Her gaze lifted to his. "Well, I don't, Mr. Jones. And I can tell I'm wasting my time appealing to your finer nature, so I'll come right to the point." She laid a manicured hand on her leather purse. "I have ten thousand dollars in cash. Leave this afternoon and you can take it with you."

He glanced at the purse. "I'm afraid that's not enough."

"Then tell me what is enough." Her voice crackled with eagerness. "I'll find a way to get it. Just say you'll leave."

He looked into her eyes. "Sorry. You couldn't pay me enough to abandon Dori to a pack of jackals like you, your husband and son. Not to mention my concern for Little Jim. Some authorities might construe what you're doing, using him as a tool to reinstate the marriage, as child abuse."

She almost spilled her beer all over her expensive beige dress. "I love that boy!"

"If that's true, which I seriously doubt, you'll help him adjust to the confusing world of divorce, instead of giving him false hope that the divorce will go away."

Tears spilled from her eyes and coursed through the artful makeup on her cheeks. She clutched her beer glass like a votive candle holder, and tears splashed into the amber liquid. "You don't understand. I need that little boy. James and I need him. When Dori had him, when he didn't live with us, I . . . I didn't feel like livin' anymore."

Tanner felt some sympathy, but not much. "Then I guess you can imagine how Dori feels. She's his mother, and she never gets to read him bedtime stories, or kiss him before he goes to sleep, or fix him his favorite breakfast, or watch Saturday-morning cartoons with him. You've stolen six months of Little Jim's childhood from her."

"But if she'd just come back . . ." Crystal choked back a sob.

Tanner took a wild guess. "Not every woman's willing to settle for a hellish marriage."

Crystal sniffed and set her beer on the end table beside her. She used the napkin to dab under her eyes. "It's not hellish."

"No?"

"There were times..." She looked away from him. "But ever since Little Jim was born, James has been a whole new person. Having that child around has made everything wonderful."

"Well, you have him back now. Why are you trying to get Dori, too?"

She glanced at him. "Jimmy Jr. wants her. He can't stand the idea that she threw him over. No girl ever did that. And L.J.—well, he really misses her. Sometimes I come up to his room, and he's got all the pictures of her spread out on his bed, and he just looks so pitiful."

"I'm sure he does."

She twisted the napkin between her fingers. "I just don't know what to do."

"Yes, you do. You just don't want to do it."

Abruptly, she stood. "I'm going to fetch him. We have to get back. James will be home any minute, and he likes to see L.J. first thing when he gets home from the office."

Tanner rose when she did. She picked up her glass of beer and carried it with her to the kitchen. She put it on the counter before she walked to the back door, opened it and called for Little Jim. The simple act of picking up after herself revealed to Tanner that she hadn't always had money. She'd obviously allowed herself to like it far too much, which made her a slave to the wishes of James Devaney, Sr. And he was Tanner's true adversary. Not Jimmy Jr., who was a coward, and not Crystal, who could still be moved to tears over the fate of her grandson. But James Devaney claimed ownership of Little Jim to satisfy his own ego without any thought to the child's welfare. Tanner realized he'd walked into the wrong office that afternoon, after all.

ALL DURING HER SHIFT Dori expected Jimmy Jr. to show up and make a scene, but finally nine o'clock arrived and he hadn't made an appearance. She could go home to Tanner. Her body quickened with anticipation as she drove the familiar route to her house. Along the way, she pulled the net from her hair and tossed it on the seat beside her.

A part of her still feared that Tanner would disappear when she wasn't looking, but his battered truck sat in her driveway. He was inside, waiting. Coming home to Tanner every night would be very special indeed. If she could come home to Tanner and Little Jim, life would be perfect.

He opened the door before she got her key in the lock and drew her into a fairyland of dancing candle flame and muted love songs on the tape player. Nudging the door closed with his foot, he gathered her close and kissed her gently. "Welcome home," he murmured. The next kiss was deeper, filled with a longing that heated her blood and sent it singing through her veins. He pushed her hair aside and nuzzled the curve of her neck. "I thought you'd never get here."

She molded her body to his. "It was the longest shift of my life."

"Then you missed me?" He leaned away from her to look into her eyes.

"Desperately."

He cupped her bottom and pressed his hips gently against her. "Is that what you missed?"

"Yes." She laced her fingers behind his neck and leaned back, keeping her pelvis locked tight with his. "But that's not all. I missed your smile, and the way you make me believe that no matter how hopeless the situation seems, it will turn out okay. I missed the way you listen to me, as if what I say really matters. I missed the sound of your voice, which has a bit of a caress in it whenever you talk to me."

He gazed at her. "That's dangerous talk, lady."

"I know," she murmured, her heart full of the emotion she didn't quite have the courage to name. Not yet.

"I hope you know where it could lead."

"I think I do."

"How about joining me at this intimate café I know, and we'll talk about it?"

"I'd love to."

He led her to the table he'd placed in the center of the living room. On it sat a beer bottle holding a candle, an uncorked bottle of wine, two unmatched stem glasses from her cupboard and a tray of crackers, cheese and fruit.

"Tanner, this is so creative."

He held her chair for her. "You have to be creative when you're on a budget."

"Are you mocking me again?"

"Absolutely not." As he scooted her forward he leaned down and kissed the side of her neck. "You've taught me what's important. I had more fun putting this together than I did going to those five-star restaurants."

"Those?" She turned her face up to his. "You've been to more than one?"

He caught her chin between his thumb and forefinger. "Yes, but I'm a changed man, Dori. Anybody can make reservations."

She smiled up at him. "No one has ever gone to this much trouble to give me a romantic evening, Tanner."

"It's only the beginning, my love."

Her heart lurched as she looked into his eyes.

He met her gaze. The endearment hadn't been carelessly tossed out. He dropped a lingering kiss on her lips before going to his chair opposite hers and sliding into it. He reached for the bottle on the table. "Wine?"

"Please." Her country-western tapes played softly in the background.

He poured a glass for each of them. Then he picked up his glass. "I remember something couples used to do when they toasted each other. I don't know if anybody ever does it anymore. They'd—"

"Link arms," Dori finished, leaning forward. "Yes. Let's."

"You wouldn't think that was overdoing it?"

"Tanner, I want to overdo it."

"Me, too."

She positioned her arm on the table, glass raised, and he leaned forward to wrap his forearm around hers.

"To us," he said.

"To us." She moved close, keeping her gaze on his as they sipped from their glasses.

He lowered his glass but didn't move away. "Give me your other hand."

She placed her left hand in his.

He twined his fingers through hers, and his gaze burned hotter than the candle flame. Her heart thumped in response.

"I want to tell you something," he said gently. "And I wish it could be the first time I'd ever said it, because then I could offer it to you brand-new and untarnished."

Her fingers tightened in his.

"Maybe you'll think it's too soon, but when something's right, time doesn't matter anymore."

She swallowed the lump in her throat. She didn't want to cry. He might not understand.

"I love you, Dori Mae Fitzpatrick."

Tears slipped down her cheeks no matter how hard she tried to hold them back and she couldn't say a word.

His gaze grew troubled. "I guess you weren't ready to hear that."

"Oh, Tanner." She choked back a sob. "I've been waiting a lifetime to hear that."

She wasn't quite sure how he managed it, but somehow her wineglass disappeared. Then he scooped her from her chair and carried her down the hall before she had a chance to protest that a man with cracked ribs shouldn't be lifting people. His lovemaking was the most exquisite experience she'd ever had as he repeated his love in a hundred ways, both spoken and unspoken.

As he entered her, she cupped his face in her hands. He paused.

"And I love you, Tanner Jones," she said.

With a groan of triumph he buried himself deep within her.

12

DORI SLEPT LIGHTLY, waking often during the night to wonder anew at her good fortune. She'd found herself a hero.

When dawn breathed the first suggestion of light into the eastern sky, she slipped out of bed carefully. The day before he'd made breakfast for her, and she would take great pleasure in returning the favor. How sweet to labor for someone you loved, she thought as she quietly took her housecoat from the bedroom closet and belted it around her. She'd forgotten the joy of giving to a man in the bitterness of Jimmy's neglect. Now her generous nature swelled with delight at the prospect of lavishing Tanner with loving care for the rest of his life.

For that's what it would be. Although marriage had not been proposed last night, Dori expected Tanner to ask her this morning. And she would accept. She paused at the doorway to Little Jim's room and gazed fondly around. Together she and Tanner would bring her son home where he belonged. He'd be able to play with his beloved Power Rangers to his heart's content. He'd— Dori's thoughts came to a halt as she realized the White Ranger wasn't on the dresser where she'd left it.

Walking into the room, she checked around and began to doubt herself. *Had* she put it on the dresser? She searched the closet, the drawers, the toy chest and under the bed. The more she looked, the more confused she became.

"Is something wrong?" Tanner asked from the doorway.

On her knees by the bed, she glanced up and her heart lurched with happiness at the thought that this wonderful man loved her. His left eye was healing nicely, and he looked tousled and rakish as he stood there wearing only his jeans.

"I woke you with all this banging around, didn't I?" she apologized.

"I've been awake since you left the bed, but you seemed to be up to something, so I played possum."

She sat back on her heels and gave him a wry smile. "I meant to bring you breakfast in bed, but I glanced in here on my way to the kitchen and now I can't find Little Jim's White Ranger. I can't imagine where it is."

Tanner frowned. "Maybe he took it outside, although I can't imagine him leaving it out there."

"That's not possible. I brought it back here after I dropped him off on Monday."

"No, I'm talking about yesterday afternoon. Your ex-mother-in-law came over and brought Little Jim with her."

"She did?" Dori pushed herself to her feet and stared at him. "Why didn't you tell me?"

"I'd planned to, but the evening was so perfect, and I figured it could wait until this morning. Nothing came of it, anyway, except that maybe Little Jim spirited his White Ranger away without my noticing."

"What did Crystal want?"

"She offered me money to leave town."

Dori gasped. "No!"

"I gathered that Little Jim is the glue holding her marriage together."

Dori sank to the bed. "She told you that?"

"Not exactly, but I could read between the lines. She needs Little Jim, but she realizes Little Jim needs you, so the obvious solution is for you and your ex to reconcile."

Dori gazed at him and marveled that she'd even considered such a thing. Slowly, she shook her head.

His eyes reflected his joy at her response. "These people are playing for keeps," he warned. "I hope you're prepared. I'm going to do everything I can, but—"

"Then it will be okay." Rising from the bed, she walked over to wrap her arms around his taped chest. She looked up into his face. "Because with a man like you, everything is a lot."

He framed her face with his hands. "We'll get him back."

"I know we will."

His mouth curved into a soft smile. "I haven't wished you good morning."

"It's not too late," she murmured, lifting her mouth for his kiss.

"Good morning, my love." He touched her lips gently at first, then proceeded with more purpose as his hands slid down her shoulders. He splayed his hand across the small of her back and molded his body to hers.

With a long sigh of pleasure she nestled close and anticipated the magic of Tanner's caress. The jangle of the telephone filled her with regret and she longed to let it ring. But it could be her parents, or even something to do with Little Jim. Slowly, she extricated herself. "Don't lose your place," she whispered before she headed for the kitchen wall phone. "It's probably somebody wanting to clean the carpet."

"I'll start the coffee," he said, following her.

She glanced at him over her shoulder before she picked up the receiver. "You're right handy to have around."

"That's the idea."

There was a smile in her voice as she answered the phone, but it quickly faded.

"Momma," came Little Jim's choked whisper, "Daddy took away my White Ranger."

Anger burned white-hot through Dori. "Don't you worry, sweetheart. We'll get him back."

"I shoulda left him with you."

"It's okay, darlin'." A warm arm curved around her shoulder and she glanced up into Tanner's concerned blue gaze. "I'll come right over. Just give me time to get dressed. I'll talk to your daddy." Would she ever.

"No!" His protest was low and urgent. "I'm not supposed to call! I'll get in trouble."

Dori reached for Tanner's hand and gripped it hard. "Your daddy's the one who will be in trouble. I—"

"Momma, you can't! They'll be really mad. Just tell Tanner I didn't lose my White Ranger. But don't come. Promise."

Helpless rage engulfed her. "But, sweetheart—"

"Please, Momma. You'll get me in trouble."

His plea tore at her heart. "Little Jim—"

"Promise!"

"Okay, but let me—" The dial tone buzzed in her ear. She replaced the receiver and faced Tanner. "Jimmy took his White Ranger."

Tanner's look of disbelief was gradually replaced with angry determination. He squeezed her shoulder. "Let's get dressed and find Devaney."

"We can't. Little Jim is petrified he'll be in trouble for calling me."

"We'll protect him, but we can't let Devaney get away with this. Come on." He started toward the bedroom.

"No."

Tanner spun around, his expression incredulous.

"I promised Little Jim we wouldn't come riding in like the cavalry. And we don't know what they might pull, when you get right down to it."

Tanner braced his hands on his hips. "So we do nothing?"

"For now." Dori met his obvious frustration with a level stare. "Look, I don't like it any more than you do."

"You've got to call a bully on his behavior or he'll just get worse."

"I promised my son I wouldn't do it. That's the end of it."

"You didn't promise I wouldn't go down and beat the stuffing out of Devaney, though, did you?"

"Tanner, stop it. It's just a battle, not the whole war. And I don't want to heap more misery on my son than I have to."

"I don't like standing around letting some son of a bitch pick on a little kid."

"Neither do I."

His defiant gaze gradually gentled. He walked back and took hold of both of her hands and drew in a deep breath. "It's time for us to present that united front we talked about. Marry me."

She looked into his eyes and found more love and compassion than she'd ever had sense enough to want in a man. "I'd be a fool not to."

Slowly, he released his breath and a grin spread across his face. "Then I passed the test?"

She smiled back. "With flying colors. And I've never known anybody who could be so creative on such a small budget."

His face became more serious and he tugged her toward the couch in the living room. "Dori, we have to talk about that."

"Why, did you cheat?" She chuckled as he led her into the living room. "What'd you do, buy expensive wine and pour it into bargain bottles?"

"No." He sat and pulled her down next to him. "But you need to know something about—"

The doorbell chimed.

She looked at him and frowned. "My house is never this busy in the morning."

"Want me to disappear?"

"Absolutely not. We have nothing to hide." She did, however, pull her housecoat more closely around her and tighten the sash before she went to the door. Through the peephole she saw Deputy Holt in uniform.

Panic took hold of her as she flung open the door and noticed his black-and-white squad car sitting at her curb. "What's happened?" she demanded of the middle-aged officer. "Is Little Jim okay?"

Deputy Holt hitched up his belt and glanced away from Dori. "He's fine, far as I know." He didn't look grief-stricken or filled with doom, just embarrassed. "I just need to talk to you for a bit."

Dori relaxed some, but she was still confused by having the deputy show up at her door first thing in the morning. "Come on in. We were about to have some coffee." It bordered on the truth. Actually, she'd decided coffee could wait until they'd celebrated their recent engagement with more earthy delights.

Deputy Holt walked into the living room, but he clearly didn't want to be there. His gaze skittered over Tanner, who had stood when the visitor entered the room. "No coffee for me, Dori," the deputy said as he pulled a notebook from his back pocket. "Thanks, anyway."

Dori crossed her arms in front of her, feeling slightly indecent despite the thickness of her housecoat. "Well, have a seat, anyway."

He remained standing. "I won't be but a minute." He glanced at Tanner again.

"Would you like me to leave the room?" Tanner asked mildly.

"Uh, no. It's on account of you that I'm here." Deputy Holt gripped a stubby pencil in his big hand as he stared down at his open notebook. "Gotta make a report."

Dori and Tanner exchanged a puzzled look. Dori faced the deputy. "A report about what?"

"Cohabitation," the deputy mumbled, not looking up.

Dori blinked. "Pardon?"

The deputy waved his pencil at Tanner. "He's been spending the night here, right?"

A chill skittered down her spine. "I—"

"Don't answer that," Tanner cut in. He stepped closer to the deputy. "That's no business of yours, officer. You're invading our privacy."

Deputy Holt glanced up at him. "Not accordin' to our county ordinance against a man and woman living together without benefit of clergy."

Dori's mouth dropped open. "You've got to be kidding."

"Wish I was. There really is an ordinance, a real old one, but it's still on the books. I looked it up."

Tanner's eyes narrowed. "Sounds like this is one of those archaic laws nobody bothers to enforce anymore."

The deputy scratched the back of his head. "Guess you could call it that. Don't ever recall anybody turning in a report like this since I've been with the sheriff's department. But nobody's voted to change it, either."

Dori felt sick to her stomach. She knew exactly who'd dug up the old ordinance and where the complaint had come from. And where it was leading. Tanner had warned her the Devaneys were playing for keeps, and nobody had ever accused them of being a stupid family.

Deputy Holt gazed at Dori, his pencil poised. "How many nights has he spent in this house?"

"You already know that." Dori lifted her chin. "I'm sure you have a report about the truck being parked in my driveway."

His gaze shifted away. "If you'll just answer the questions, Dori Mae, this will go easier."

Tanner cleared his throat. "I've spent two nights here because I wasn't feeling well after being attacked Tuesday night and I have no friends in Los Lobos besides Dori. But she and I have not shared a bed or had any sexual relations. That's what you really want to know, isn't it?"

Tanner's willingness to tell an officer of the law such a blatant lie for her sake was stunning. She dared not look at him for fear her shocked gratitude would show.

"That's the gist of it," the deputy said. He sent Tanner a piercing look. "You'd be willing to swear to that under oath?"

Tanner made an impatient noise and turned away.

"Is that the truth of it, Dori Mae?" Deputy Holt asked her.

She swallowed. "Yes."

He flipped his notebook closed. "Now that you're up and about, Jones, I'd suggest you get yourself back to the motel."

Tanner didn't reply.

Dori forced herself to be polite as she walked Deputy Holt to the door and opened it for him. After she closed the door she leaned against it and stared at Tanner, her eyes filling with tears. "You'll have to move back to the motel."

"The hell I will. I'm calling my lawyer."

"*Your* lawyer? Now you're sounding like one of the Devaneys!" She squeezed her eyes shut.

"It's time to fight fire with fire."

"We don't have any fire!" She opened her eyes. "Which is just fine with me. I hate the way money makes people act. They buy the sheriff! They buy the judge! Money corrupts people, Tanner. We're lucky not to have it."

He regarded her steadily. "It's not the money. It's the way they use it. Money's not bad in itself."

"Yes, it is! Have you ever watched the difference between people with money and people without it? The ones with money act as if they can have anything they want. Nope. I don't want a thing to do with a person who has lots of money. Give me plain, honest, hardworking people any day."

He rubbed the back of his neck and glanced at her. Then he sighed deeply. "So you want me to move back to the motel?"

"Just for now, Tanner. I can see the Devaneys are trying to build a case for my being an unfit mother, and I don't want to give them any more ammunition than they already have."

"Getting married would solve the problem."

"I know, but that will take time to plan." She saw the impatience in his eyes. "I know we could go to Vegas, like you said before, but my parents would be crushed. I want to do this right, Tanner. No rusty nails or warped boards."

"All right." He started toward the bedroom and turned back. "When will I see you again?"

"If you'll pick me up after work tonight, we could go out for a bite and start making our plans."

"At the café or here?"

She hesitated. "Here, I guess. Then I'll have a chance to change clothes."

He nodded, still watching her. Then, with a muttered oath, he strode over and kissed her until she was breathless.

"Goodness, Tanner," she said, gasping as her body pounded with desire. "How am I supposed to send you away after that?"

His smile was devilish as he fondled her breast. "You're not. But don't worry about it. I'm leaving. I just want to make sure you miss me after I go."

TANNER HATED THE IDEA of abandoning Dori and moving back into the motel, but in some ways it was a good move. He needed some thinking room, and he didn't get much of that when he was tempted by Dori's charms.

She was hopelessly prejudiced about wealth, and he'd have to approach the subject of his money very carefully. Before the untimely arrival of Deputy Holt he'd thought the mood was exactly right to broach the subject. But once Dori had been reminded of the evils that could be perpetrated by money, she was in no frame of mind to hear about his considerable holdings.

As he'd learned in business, timing was everything. Once she'd had a chance to be apart from him for several hours and miss the closeness they'd discovered to be so essential to both of them, once he'd made love to her again, in the bed of the old truck if necessary, he'd tell her. Then maybe, just maybe, her prejudice would be softened enough by love to allow him to convince her he wouldn't rule her life the way Jimmy Jr. had done.

In the meantime, he had some business to conduct. Elmer had been pleased, though confused, when Tanner presented himself and asked if number nine was still available. Dumb luck had been at work and the room was empty.

From the privacy of his room, he contacted his lawyers. Fortunately, he hadn't slipped and let on to Dori that he had more than one. He wanted his legal team up and ready when the time came, so he discussed the custody case with them and asked them to research similar cases and find all the established precedents.

"Finally going to marry somebody, Tanner?" asked Franklin, the senior partner in the firm.

"If she'll have me."

"With your net worth?" Franklin chuckled. "I can't picture a woman turning that down. In addition to obtaining the bonus of your winning personality, of course."

"Would you believe she doesn't want anything to do with a rich guy?"

"Then marry the lady, Tanner. She sounds like a perfect candidate for that prenuptial agreement we have gathering dust in the files."

"Right." Tanner felt an unexplainable twinge at the thought of asking Dori to sign the agreement. But he'd sworn never to marry anyone unless they agreed to leave his business alone in the event of a divorce. Romance was one thing. Business was another. He wouldn't try to control Dori with the power of his wealth, but he certainly didn't want to be vulnerable to having his business chopped in half if everything went sour. After all, this was the nineties. People started out with great hopes, but in the end, one in three marriages ended in divorce.

Yet somehow the thought of that prenuptial agreement depressed the hell out of him. It was insurance, and he definitely wanted it. Any man in his position would expect that sort of cooperation from the woman he intended to marry. Dori didn't want money, anyway, so she'd probably gladly sign away her rights to his fortune. Gladly sign away, if she agreed to marry him in the first place, once she found out his financial status.

Tanner thought about the love in Dori's eyes when he'd caressed her the night before and was sure they could overcome this little problem between them. Then he considered the disdain in her expression when she talked about the evils of money, and his confidence evaporated.

13

IN ALL HER YEARS of working at the Double Nickel, Dori had never known Crystal Devaney to set foot in the place. Yet in the middle of the afternoon, Crystal's blue Caddy pulled up in front of the café. The car didn't look any more comfortable in a lot full of pickups than Crystal did in her green linen suit as she pushed through the door of the Double Nickel and stood looking around at truckers in Western shirts and baseball caps. Men such as these provided Crystal with her designer clothes and late-model luxury cars, but she'd stayed as removed from their labor as a princess ignoring the duties of her stable boys.

As Dori watched, coffee carafe in hand, Crystal hesitated and finally made her way to a stool at the far end of the counter. Dori concluded that Crystal had made this pilgrimage to talk to her, a possibility Dori met with mixed emotions. She saw a woman struggling to build a life in the face of training that had doomed her to heartbreak, yet Crystal had worked harder than anyone to deprive Dori of her son once the divorce had become official.

And Crystal continued to connive to get what she wanted. Just the day before she'd tried to bribe Tanner. Dori tempered her natural compassion with that re-

minder as she set the carafe on a burner and approached
Crystal, an order pad in her hand.

"May I help you with something, Crystal?"

"I came to talk to you."

Dori cast an eye over her customers. Nobody seemed
desperately in need of attention, so she drew closer to her
ex-mother-in-law. "It's no good, you know. I just can't
see myself going back to Jimmy."

Crystal picked up a sugar packet and tore the corner
off. She poured the sugar in a neat pyramid on the
counter. "You're a stubborn girl, Dori Mae." She glanced
up from the pile of sugar. "But you're in over your head.
When I failed with your boyfriend, I turned the matter
over to James."

Dori should have expected it. Crystal always resorted
to her husband's power when the going got tough. "So
that's when he dug out that old ordinance and set the
sheriff's department on us."

Crystal trained her green-eyed gaze on Dori. "James
can use the information he has to make a case for immoral conduct. He will if he has to, and he'll eliminate
your visitation rights completely."

"Even you and James wouldn't do that to Little Jim."
Dori prayed it was true.

"It would be very sad, but how long can L.J. live torn
between two worlds? James says maybe it's better to cut
it off clean."

Dori felt very cold. "Is that what you think, Crystal?
You're a mother. You still sneak money to your daugh-
ter. James wanted to cut that off clean after she left for
L.A., but you couldn't do it, any more than I could have.
You continue to care for Libby, even if James doesn't."

"James cares." Crystal flattened the sugar pyramid with deliberate motions of her forefinger. "But he's practical, too." She glanced up. "If you're not afraid of losing visitation with Little Jim, think of your boyfriend."

"He's already been beaten up. What's left? Surely James wouldn't stoop to murder."

"Economic murder," Crystal said quietly. "I heard him talking to Jimmy Jr. He's already started contacting people around the state. He could have your young man blackballed so he won't be able to get a construction job in the entire state of Texas. I could still stop that from happening, but you'd have to agree to send him out of town today. Within the hour."

Dori's insides turned to jelly. Blackballed. What an ugly concept.

"And a man with a bad record in Texas might have a tough time getting a job wherever he goes. Reputations follow people around, you know," Crystal added for good measure.

The fight went out of Dori. It seemed that whenever she tried to fix the mistake she'd made in marrying Jimmy, someone she loved ended up getting hurt. Little Jim was petrified of reprisals, and Tanner wasn't afraid, but he darn well should be. He'd been very brave until now, but he hadn't been faced with unemployment. That should change his tune.

"Tell him to leave by five this afternoon," Crystal said. "James won't put out the word if he's gone by five."

"Did James send you to tell me that?"

"I offered to go. James said it would do no good, that the two of you were bent on self-destruction, but I thought differently. I wanted you both to have a chance to change your minds before James rolled over you."

Dori looked into her eyes. "I'll tell him to leave. I don't know if he will."

"Why can't you just give in and come back?" Crystal asked, clearly perplexed by Dori's behavior.

"Because I don't want to end up like you," Dori said. Then she carefully wiped up the spilled sugar.

DORI TRIED TANNER several times at the Prairie Schooner and was told by Elmer that the line was busy. The concept of Tanner tying up the phone lines gave Dori pause. She wondered if he was calling family members to get support for his position or to ask advice. He'd presented himself as such a lone wolf that the idea of him gathering wisdom from friends and relatives altered her concept of Tanner Jones.

Finally at four-thirty she managed to get through. "James Devaney is prepared to blackball you if you don't leave town by five tonight," she said. "I believe he can do it. You'll never work construction in Texas again."

To her amazement he laughed. "That's what he thinks," Tanner said. "Bring him on."

"You're being completely foolish." She heard the note of hysteria in her voice but there wasn't much she could do about it. The man she'd come to love in the past few days was about to commit financial suicide, and she couldn't bear to watch. "If you can't earn a living, we won't have enough money to fight for custody of Little Jim," she reminded him. Desperation drove her to cruelty. "I don't want a man who can't hold up his end."

"I'll hold it up, Dori."

"You don't know what you're facing. If you love me, you'll leave town right now. Do it for me, if you won't do it for yourself."

There was a long silence on the other end.

"Tanner, are you there?" she asked at last.

"Dori, I'm not leaving town before our date tonight. When we have a chance to talk, you'll understand."

"But by that time you'll be dead in the water!"

"The White Ranger doesn't give up that easily," he said softly.

"What?" She felt a sob lodge in her throat. "Listen, you crazy guy. Cartoons are not real life. You've proved that you're a hero. Now ride out of here, okay?"

"See you at the end of your shift, Dori."

"Tanner—" She replaced the receiver when she realized he was no longer at the other end.

By eight that night the café was buzzing and Dori raced from booths to counter, taking care of the crowd as country tunes blasted from the jukebox.

The cook shoved an order across the pass-through. "When you deliver that, somebody's waiting by the back door for you," he said. "Better hurry."

A wave of misery engulfed her as she took the plate and carried it to a booth. Tanner had decided to leave, after all, but he'd waited too long. James Devaney's spies would have informed him that Tanner had missed the five o'clock deadline. After delivering the order, she hurried through the kitchen and out the back door of the café, expecting to see Tanner's truck parked there.

Instead, she discovered James Devaney leaning against the fender of his black Cadillac. She recoiled as if she'd caught sight of a rattlesnake. The stench of garbage from a nearby Dumpster was highly appropriate, she thought.

"Hello, Dori Mae." He sounded almost friendly.

"What are you doing here?"

James folded his arms across his chest. He looked extremely pleased with himself. "I just received a piece of information that I thought you might be interested in hearing."

"I suppose all the big construction companies in the state have agreed never to hire Tanner Jones again." She shook her head. "You have a funny way of trying to win me over, James."

"Crystal tells me you have a strange aversion to men with money."

Dori clenched her fists at her sides. "You and Jimmy have taught me that rich men are into power. I have this thing about keeping my independence."

"So you're looking for someone poor, then?"

Dori's laugh was bitter. "I know what comes next. You've made certain Tanner will be extremely poor, haven't you? Well, let me tell you something. Tanner will survive. You may have messed him up temporarily, but you haven't broken his spirit. He's twice the man you'll ever be, and he'll be fine."

James stroked his chin as he gazed at her. "I imagine he will survive. As the owner of one of the most successful construction companies in East Texas, he should continue to do very well."

AT NINE-THIRTY that night Tanner pulled into Dori's driveway. He'd borrowed Elmer and Beatrice's picnic basket and stocked it with wine, cold cuts and cheese for a picnic out on some star-spangled country road. He figured they'd eat in the back of the pickup, and the blanket he'd brought along could serve for the other activity he had in mind for tonight.

The simple and inexpensive meal was only one way he planned to demonstrate how little he cared for the trappings of a monied existence. Yet he had to convince Dori that wealth could be used for a good cause, namely to restore Little Jim to her. But first he wanted to make love to her and reestablish the bond between them.

He parked the truck, but before he could climb out, Dori came out the front door and walked quickly toward the truck. He was gratified that she'd been watching for him and was apparently eager to spend the rest of the evening in his company, but he was surprised that she hadn't changed out of her waitressing uniform. Leaping from the cab, he came around to open the passenger door for her.

His smile of welcome faded at the expression on her face. "What's wrong?"

She flung him a look of utter loathing. "The only reason I'm getting into this truck with you is because I might start shouting, and I don't want to disturb the neighbors."

"Dori, what—"

"Get in and drive, Tanner. Go out somewhere in the fields, where nobody can hear us."

He closed her door and came around to the driver's seat. Only one thing could have created this level of rage in her. Dammit to hell. "You found out, didn't you?" he asked as he closed his door.

"I don't want to talk about it here."

She had found out. He was certain of it. This was the risk he'd taken by not telling her earlier, but he'd been so close to the right moment. So damn close. He drove the rattletrap old truck out of her subdivision and headed for open cotton fields while she sat fuming beside him. A couple of times he glanced at her rigid profile and cursed softly to himself.

Finally, he swung the truck onto a dirt road that ran off to the left from the two-lane blacktop. He cut the motor and cracked the window, letting in the scent of freshly turned earth and the chirp of crickets. He turned to her.

She, however, did not turn toward him. Instead, she stared out the bug-spattered windshield. "The thing I can't figure out is why you pretended to be poor in the first place. You had no way of knowing that was so important to me."

"I'd planned to tell you all that tonight."

She faced him then, her eyes shining with tears. "Oh, were you? Why should I believe that?" Her voice rose a notch. "Why should I believe anything you say, come to think of it?"

"Because I love you." It was one of two aces he held.

"Don't, Tanner." Tears spilled down her cheeks. "Love is about honesty, not lies!"

He reached for her, but she pulled away. That hurt more than anything. If he couldn't hold her close while he explained this, she wouldn't buy it. She'd trumped one of his aces.

"Whose truck is this, anyway?" she asked, swiping the tears from her cheeks.

"It belongs to one of my employees."

"This was all a deliberate plan, wasn't it? To pretend to be a hand-to-mouth construction worker?"

"Yes." He thought how much she looked like the picture she'd sent him, her brown eyes wide and vulnerable, her full lips slightly parted. He'd never wanted her more than at this moment. Yet he didn't dare touch her.

"Why did you pretend all that?" she asked.

He sighed. "Because I wanted to make sure the woman I married wanted me and not my money."

"Oh, Tanner." She buried her face in her hands. "I can't believe everything has turned out this way."

Frustration roughened his voice. "You wouldn't have given me the time of day if I'd been honest!"

"No, and we both would have saved a lot of effort!" She sent him a withering glance. "Lying never works out, Tanner."

"I didn't like the lying part, either, and I would have told you sooner, but you kept raving about the evils of money."

"It *is* evil."

"No, it's not. Just because you've had one bad experience—"

"Which made me look around, and see how the world works. Money separates people, putting them on different levels. Now I understand why you asked me about being a waitress. That would hardly be appropriate for your wife, would it?"

"Dori, if you wanted to work as an elephant trainer after we're married, I wouldn't stop you."

"But you see, we won't be getting married."

He'd tried to prepare himself for her rejection during the drive out here, but it still hit him like an iron girder in the gut. "Please don't say that. At least listen to what—"

"Save your breath, Tanner. I won't put myself in that position again, where the man has all the power and I have none."

He wanted to grab her and kiss her until she listened to reason, but he gripped the steering wheel instead. "That's bull. I won't tell you what to do any more than a poor man would. Just because you had that experience with Jimmy, don't lump all rich men in together. That's not fair."

Her brown gaze softened a fraction. "I know you're not like Jimmy. You wouldn't mean to throw your weight around, but it would happen, just the same. If you're bringing all that money into the family, then your doings would automatically become more important than mine. When I was married to Jimmy we had visitors at the Devaneys, couples in the same income bracket as Crystal and James, and it was always the same. The women were coddled, patted on the head and dismissed like children."

He hit the steering wheel with the flat of his hand. "I wouldn't do that, dammit!"

"Oh, wouldn't you?"

"No."

"If we got married, where would we live?"

"Somewhere near Dallas. I mean, that's where my business . . ." He paused as he realized what he was saying. She didn't even have to point it out. She'd talked about how much she loved the Texas plains, and yet he'd ignored her needs because it would be very inconvenient to live in Los Lobos and try to conduct business in Dallas.

"That's only the beginning, Tanner. You'll just assume those decisions are yours to make, because after all, you own this big successful company. I don't even blame you for feeling that way. I just don't want to be the little wife tucked away at home."

Which is exactly what he wanted, if he were completely honest with himself. The thought made him very uncomfortable. Desperate to turn events in his favor, he hauled out his other ace. "I could use my money to get Little Jim back."

She took a long, shaky breath. "Don't think I haven't thought of that."

"I thought that was your original goal."

"It was."

"Then what's the problem? I have lawyers who can make mincemeat of the Devaneys. Marry me and they'll be at your disposal."

She gazed down at her hands that were clenched tightly in her lap. "Oh, but you do tempt me, Mr. Jones."

Hope flared and he covered her hands with one of his. "Be tempted, Dori. I promise to make you the happiest woman in the world."

When she looked up the sadness in her eyes took his breath away. "I thought you didn't want a woman who married you for your money," she said.

He stared at her.

"That's what I'd be doing, Tanner. And believe me, I've considered it. Missing Little Jim like I do, I'll admit that sometimes I've thought about going back to Jimmy just to get my son back. And now I could marry you for the same reason. I wish I could do that. But I can't."

The pain in his heart was so great he wondered how he'd stand it. He squeezed her hand, which was cold beneath his. "Dori—"

"I would become just like Crystal. I understand now that she sacrificed herself to keep her family together, but you see, it backfired. She's given her children a weak role model. Her daughter's out in California trying to build some self-respect after years of having none, and Jimmy's growing up to treat women just like his father always has." Her chin lifted and resolution flashed in her eyes. "My son will have a different role model for a mother."

Tanner ground his teeth together. "How can I convince you that I won't use my money to control you?"

Her gaze was filled with tragic certainty. "You can't. Now please take me home."

His throat hurt. "You said you loved me."

"I loved Tanner Jones, the construction worker. I don't know who you are."

He searched her face for the slightest sign that would encourage him to gather her into his arms. There was none. Dazed by loss, he started the truck and headed back toward Los Lobos.

They drove in silence toward her house. When they were two blocks away he sat up straighter at the sight of a black-and-white cruiser and a black Caddy parked in front of Dori's house.

"Oh, my God," Dori whispered.

Tanner pressed down on the gas and in seconds screeched to a stop in front of the house. Dori leapt from the cab before he'd turned off the motor. She ran to the lawn where James, Jimmy and Crystal Devaney stood with Deputy Holt.

Tanner loped over toward them, his gut clenched. "What's happened?"

James Devaney turned to him. His hair was wildly out of place and his shirt was only half-tucked into his pants. His voice came out a hoarse croak. "L.J.'s missing."

14

TANNER'S ATTENTION FLEW to Dori, who looked as if she might pass out. He stepped close to her and put a bracing arm around her waist. "When did you discover he was gone?"

"About an hour ago." Crystal's voice was choked with tears, and without makeup and the clever cut of designer clothes she looked her age. "For some reason I decided to check on him, and he wasn't in his room. James and I tore all through the house, but he wasn't there. Then we thought he might be with Jimmy, but Jimmy came home and hadn't seen him. That's when we called Deputy Holt."

During Crystal's explanation, Dori had slid her hand down to clutch Tanner's. He gave her hand a reassuring squeeze. "We'll find him," he murmured close to her ear.

"Does he have a key to your house?" the deputy asked Dori.

"No." She swallowed. "But let's go look inside, anyway. Maybe he found a way to get in. Maybe he's asleep in his bed."

Tanner hoped so. Unfortunately, the Devaneys had enough money to make kidnapping for ransom a very real possibility. He figured Dori had already thought of that, too. Another reason for her to hate those with money.

Dori fumbled with the lock but eventually opened the door. Everyone spread out to search the house and call out for the boy. There was no answer.

"Let's try the yard," Dori said, heading for the back door.

Once again everyone searched and called, but the backyard was silent except for a breeze through the large oak tree in the corner of the yard.

"I'm going out to the cruiser and radio for backup," Deputy Holt said. "I'll need one of you to go back to the Devaney house in case he shows up there, and somebody should stay here, for the same reason. The rest of you can start driving around the area. We'll find him."

"Crystal will stay at our house," James said. "Jimmy and I will go out and search."

"Good." Deputy Holt's glance flicked to Tanner and Dori.

Tanner stepped forward. "I'll search."

"No. I want to search," said Dori.

He looked back at her. He didn't know what evil was out there, and he could be putting her in danger, but a newborn instinct guided him to agree. "Okay, I'll stay here." Her expression of gratitude told him he'd made the right decision.

Deputy Holt seemed skeptical, but he didn't comment on Dori's decision to join the search party. "I'll check back at the Devaney house every ten minutes," he said, heading for the door. "If anybody finds him, call there."

"I'll get my keys," Dori said.

Within seconds Tanner was alone in the house, and as he paced from room to room, he realized why Dori had been so determined to search. The passive role he'd agreed to take on didn't sit well. Tanner recalled how James had arbitrarily claimed the active role for himself and his son and Crystal hadn't even blinked. After years of training, she wouldn't. But Tanner chafed under the restriction of being the one waiting at home.

If he smoked, he'd do it now, but he'd given that up years ago. He didn't want to have a beer and risk blurring his reaction time by even a fraction of a second. Finally, he decided to roam the backyard for a while. He'd circled the perimeter of the block wall and had paused to lean against Little Jim's swing set when he thought he heard a noise. He listened more carefully and decided he was imagining things.

On his way back inside he heard it again, a faint rustling in the branches of the oak tree. Probably a squirrel, he thought, but he crossed the yard, anyway. He stood under the tree and peered up into the shadowy branches. Gradually, his vision sharpened. Little Jim was huddled there.

"Taking orders from Mighty Morphin?" Tanner asked gently.

"Hi, Tanner."

"Everybody's out looking for you."

"I know. I thought Momma would stay here, but then you did."

"And what would you have done if your momma had stayed instead of me?"

The leaves rustled again as Little Jim shifted his position. "I woulda come down and told her we had to run away."

"And why's that?"

After a long silence Little Jim replied. "I heard Daddy and Grandpa say they're gonna fix it so Momma can't have Mondays anymore."

Tanner's heart ached as he imagined the desperation Little Jim must have felt when he overheard that conversation. And he'd shown great courage in making his way through the dark night to warn his mother. He'd obviously learned that courage from Dori. "We won't let them take you away from your momma," he said.

"You can stop them?" Little Jim sounded as if he wanted to believe, but he'd probably been disappointed too many times in his young life to accept whatever Tanner told him.

"Yes."

"How?"

"By hiring the best lawyers in the country."

"Oh." His sigh of defeat filtered down through the leaves. "But Momma and me, we don't have much money."

"I do."

Little Jim's gasp of surprise nearly made him topple from the tree. "You do?"

"Yes, and I'm going to help your momma fight this."

"You sure don't act rich."

Tanner smiled grimly. "Thanks. Say, Jim, I'm getting a stiff neck from looking up into this tree. Any chance you're ready to climb down?"

"Yeah. I hafta go to the bathroom, anyway."

Tanner helped the boy down from the tree and they walked together into the house. "I need to call your grandma and tell her you're okay," Tanner said as Little Jim scampered down the hall toward the bathroom.

Little Jim skidded to a halt and looked back at Tanner. "You promise they won't do that to Momma?"

"I promise." Tanner didn't know if Dori would ever marry him, but if she were faced with losing all contact with her son, she'd probably accept the loan of his lawyers. He'd make sure they gave her a reduced fee, because she'd probably want to pay the entire cost even if it took her the rest of her life.

"Then you can tell Grandma I'm here."

Tanner made the call. Once Crystal understood that her grandson was safe she began to sob, but Tanner was unmoved. "He decided to run away because he overheard your husband and son talking about denying Dori visitation privileges," he said.

"Oh, God."

"I suggest the three of you rethink your position with regard to that little boy."

She choked back another sob. "James gets so determined."

"And how about you? Is there any backbone left after thirty years of subjugation?"

The silence was filled with her sniffling. "I don't know," she said at last.

RED AND BLUE LIGHTS whirled in Dori's rearview mirror. She pulled off the road, shot out of the car and ran back toward the cruiser. "Any news?"

The young deputy who'd only been in uniform about six months looked proud to deliver the message. "Found him, Dori Mae. He's at your house, safe and sound."

Dori put out a hand to steady herself against the roof of the car and closed her eyes as the world began to spin. Thank God. Oh, thank God.

"You okay?"

His words galvanized her. "I'm fine," she said, opening her eyes again. "Thank you. Thank you very much."

"Want a police escort to your house?"

"Absolutely."

She raced for her car and nearly flooded the engine in her eagerness to get moving. Gravel spurted from beneath her tires as she charged back onto the road and the cruiser had to put on a burst of speed to get ahead of her. She rode his bumper and beeped her horn for him to go faster, despite the fact they were exceeding the speed limit by at least twenty miles an hour.

"Come on," she muttered, landing on the horn again. "Come on."

She arrived just ahead of the black Caddy that brought Crystal, James and Jimmy. She beat them into the house and Little Jim ran into her arms. She noticed through a blur of tears that he was wearing his Power Rangers T-shirt.

"Momma, Tanner's gonna help us!" Little Jim said as he pulled away and looked into her face. "He's rich!"

Dori glanced up from where she'd crouched down to hug Little Jim.

Tanner stood just beyond her son, his gaze intense. "I guess some people don't have a problem with that."

"Neither did I when I was five years old," she said. "But I'm all grown up now."

"L.J.?" Crystal called from the open front door. "Where are you, honey?"

"Right here, Grandma." Little Jim tightened his grip around Dori's neck.

He was really too big to pick up, but Dori did it, anyway, holding him tight as she stood and faced Crystal, James and Jimmy. She glared at the three of them.

James stepped forward as if to take Little Jim from her, but Tanner moved to block his path.

"I'd keep my hands off that boy if I were you," Tanner said.

"Out of my way, Jones," the older man said. "Jimmy, let's take your son home."

"My lawyers have filed a suit in Dori's name against the two of you for conspiring to deprive this boy of his mother," Tanner said. "I'd tread lightly from here on out, or you may prejudice the case even more. Little Jim ran away from home because he was unhappy. He wants to stay here tonight. I've talked to a judge who says that's just fine. He'll be glad to issue a restraining order against all three of you if that becomes necessary."

James swung back to the door where Deputy Holt stood. "What's going on here, Holt?"

"I'm sorry, Mr. Devaney, but it's just like he said," the deputy replied. "I checked on it. You'd better leave Little Jim here for the time being."

"The hell I will. Jimmy, get L.J. and we'll be on our way. It's late."

Dori clutched her son, who buried his face against her neck. Tanner flexed his shoulders and Deputy Holt looked very worried.

"James, leave L.J. be." Crystal's voice was soft but laced with a determination Dori had never heard from her former mother-in-law.

James Devaney turned slowly, slack jawed with disbelief as he stared at his wife.

She met his incredulity with a steady gaze. Her voice gained power as she spoke. "We've allowed our selfishness to make that little boy's life miserable, and it's going to stop now."

James cleared his throat. "Crystal, honey, you've been under a strain. I'll handle this."

"I haven't been under a strain. I've been under your thumb."

"Oh, for crying out loud, Crystal."

She squared her shoulders and drew in a breath. "I thought it would be hard to buck you, but it's not that hard, after all. I love our grandson, and I won't stand by and watch you and Jimmy frighten him with stories about taking him away from his momma. I'll go to the mat with you on this, James."

James's eyes narrowed. "Is that a threat?"

"Take it however you want. Besides, Dori has a champion now." Crystal waved a hand in Tanner's direction. "From what I hear about him, he could drag you through the courts until all your money is gone. You may be stubborn, James, but you're not stupid enough to risk your entire fortune. It's time to throw in the towel and give Dori custody of L.J."

Veins pulsed at his temples and his face reddened. "Over my dead body!"

Crystal stared him down. "With your high blood pressure, you'd better calm down, or that's exactly how it will happen. Now let's go home. As you said, it's late."

James glanced to his son for support, but Jimmy Jr. only shrugged. Dori wasn't surprised. Jimmy followed whoever was leading, and right now that person was Crystal.

James turned back to Dori and shook a finger in her face. "Don't think this is the end of it, Dori Mae."

Dori didn't respond, but her heart sang with relief because it was the end of it. James Devaney's reign of terror was over. Just like that, Crystal had called his bluff and found that she held more control than she'd ever imagined. It also didn't hurt that she had Tanner Jones to hold over her husband's head.

Deputy Holt followed the Devaneys out, and Dori heard him apologizing the length of the walkway. Something about Mr. Jones having friends in high places leading all the way up to the governor's office, and the sheriff's hands being tied.

Tanner closed the door and Dori finally relaxed enough to ease Little Jim to the floor.

Her son gazed up at her. "I can stay here tonight?"

Dori gave him a shaky smile. She was almost afraid to believe it. "I think you'll be able to stay here every night."

"Really?"

Dori nodded and fought tears.

Little Jim hugged her hard. "That's good, Momma."

"Yes, it's good." She smoothed his red curls with trembling fingers. Then she looked at Tanner standing across the room by the door. "Thank you," she said around a lump in her throat.

"Crystal's the one you should thank," he said.

"I will, but I don't know if she would have stood up to James if you hadn't put the pressure on her in the first place."

"Momma?" Little Jim looked up at her, an impish gleam in his eyes. "Can I stay up and watch TV and eat popcorn because it's a special night?"

Dori gazed on her precious, freckle-faced son and was so filled with love she could scarcely speak. But he counted on her to be his mother, and she took the job very seriously. She tugged on his earlobe. "A special night? You scared the wits out of a lot of people who love you. You're lucky you aren't grounded, buddy."

"Then I can't stay up late?"

"You're already up late. Now go in and get your pajamas on and brush your teeth. Call when you're ready and I'll tuck you in." Her voice quivered on the last part of that statement. Tonight she would have the privilege of tucking Little Jim in his bed. She would never take that privilege for granted again.

"Okay." Little Jim dragged himself down the hallway.

"If you're a very good boy tomorrow, we can see about some TV and popcorn tomorrow night," she called after him.

"Okay!" He skipped the rest of the way into his bedroom.

Dori faced Tanner. The faint scent of his woodsy after-shave drifted toward her, beckoning her closer. She held her ground. "I don't know what to say. You've been wonderful, more than wonderful."

His blue eyes filled with resignation. "But it doesn't change anything, does it?"

She shook her head.

"You realize you're an impossibly pigheaded, prejudiced woman? What do you want me to do, give it all away?"

"Of course not." She called on her last reserves of strength and somehow found the words she had to say. "I want you to go back to that bushel basket of letters you got from the article in *Texas Men* and find a woman who's delighted to be the little wife of a very rich man. I'm sure there's someone out there like that." She didn't allow herself to think of Tanner with another woman. The picture of him holding someone else might make her start screaming.

"I'm sure there are women out there like that. And I happened to run into the one woman in the entire world who thinks *money* is a dirty word!" He braced his hands on his hips and stared at a point over her shoulder. Finally, his gaze moved back to her face. His voice was husky. "I love you. Doesn't that count for anything?"

Her throat tightened. "That's what makes this the most difficult decision I've made in my life. But I will not live like a kept woman, Tanner."

"Dammit, you would not be a kept woman!"

"When a waitress marries a CEO, that's the way it turns out, in my experience. I don't believe in the Cinderella story anymore. I'm sorry." She took a deep breath. "More sorry than I can say."

He stood looking at her, his throat working. "That's it, then." He reached in his back pocket and pulled out a card. "If the Devaneys don't cooperate in the custody case, get in touch with me."

She took the embossed card, careful not to touch his fingers. "I will."

"Dori—"

"Go, Tanner." She hurt all over. "Before we both break down and Little Jim comes in to find out what's wrong. He's had enough trauma for one night."

He turned and walked quietly out the door.

15

TWO DAYS LATER, while Dori and Little Jim were watching the Power Rangers on Saturday-morning cartoons, a parcel arrived in the overnight mail for Little Jim. Dori saw the return address and her stomach clenched. Most of the time she'd been able to keep thoughts of Tanner at bay by concentrating on her son, but seeing his handwriting on the package brought an image of his hand holding the pen, the same hand that had touched her so lovingly.

"Who's it from, Momma?" Little Jim hopped up and down in his excitement over the unexpected delivery.

"From Tanner." She handed him the box. "For you."

Little Jim sat down right where he was and started fumbling with the box. "I can't open it, Momma."

"I'll get the scissors." She helped him open the box and stepped back to let him enjoy unveiling the contents all by himself. She wasn't surprised when he pulled out a new White Ranger.

He let out a whoop of joy and hugged the toy to his chest. "I've got my White Ranger back, Momma! Tanner got him back. And he cleaned him up, too!" His green eyes shone with happiness.

Dori decided not to point out that this was a different White Ranger. She'd learned from Crystal that Jimmy Jr. had destroyed the original one. Crystal had offered to replace it, but Dori had asked her to hold off. It would be just like Tanner to send a new one, Dori thought, and she didn't want Little Jim to become confused by getting two. And sure enough, Tanner had come through. Dori pressed a hand to her heart as if that could ease the aching there.

"Let's clean up the mess," she said, stooping to pick up the box. A note fell out. Little Jim's name was on the outside. "Looks like Tanner sent you a message," she said.

"Can you read it to me?"

Of course Tanner would have known that Little Jim hadn't learned to read and she'd have to help out with the note. He wanted her to read his message and think of him. Doggone his cleverness. She opened the note with shaking fingers and started to read out loud.

Dear Jim,
The White Ranger insisted on staying with you because he says you're the kind of guy he'd like to have on his team. He thinks you're very brave, and so do I. I think your mother's very brave, too. Tell her hello for me.

                                                                Love, Tanner

Little Jim clutched his toy close as he gazed up at his mother. "When's Tanner coming back, Momma?"

Dori pressed her lips together and swallowed hard. "He won't be coming back, sweetheart."

"Momma, you're crying!"

"No. I just got something in my eye." She grabbed a tissue from the pocket of her jeans and blew her nose. Then she turned toward the television. "Hey, we're missing our show!"

IN THE NEXT TWO WEEKS Crystal amazed Dori with her efficient handling of the custody matter. She'd explained to Dori that James wasn't much good at backing down, so he'd washed his hands of the whole thing. Crystal worked with a lawyer and had a new agreement written.

One Saturday morning early in November, Crystal appeared at Dori's house with a copy of the tentative agreement. Dori offered her a cup of coffee and she accepted. They sat at Dori's kitchen table, and while Dori scanned the agreement, Crystal enjoyed a view of Little Jim and his friends playing on the swing set in the backyard. As she watched him play and commented fondly on his good coordination and cheerful nature, Dori realized with surprise that Crystal had become a friend. The week before she'd invited Crystal to go trick-or-treating with her and Little Jim and Crystal had shown up for the event in a fairy godmother costume.

"Do these terms sound fair to you?" Crystal asked. She looked apprehensive as she waved her hand at the agreement her lawyer had drawn up.

"I think they sound very fair." The agreement gave her custody of Little Jim, and the Devaneys had visitation rights every other weekend.

"After what's happened, you're very generous to allow us this much."

"I would never want Little Jim to lose contact with his daddy and his grandparents."

Crystal looked very relieved. "Then I guess we're ready to set up a hearing."

"Fine. I'd like to get it settled." Dori got up and went over to the counter where she picked up a packet of snapshots. "I had a set of Halloween pictures made for you."

"Oh! Let me see!" Crystal reached for them eagerly and lingered over each shot, chuckling at Little Jim in his White Ranger outfit standing next to her in her fairy godmother costume. "These are terrific. They're going right up on the refrigerator."

"I thought they were good, too."

"I hope we can get the hearing over with by Thanksgiving, so it doesn't muddy up the holidays. I can't believe it's the ninth of November already."

"Is it? What do you know." Dori hadn't taken note of the date. But she wasn't likely to have anything particularly unusual happen to her today. The baby-sitter would arrive at twelve-thirty and she'd go to work. Then she'd come home and she and Little Jim would have popcorn and watch television, a privilege she still treasured, but which wasn't out of the ordinary now.

Crystal tucked the pictures into the envelope and put them in the purse she'd hung over the back of her chair. "Those snapshots are wonderful. I think it was seeing those walls of pictures in your bedroom the night Little Jim disappeared that made up my mind for me. That was heart-wrenching."

Dori slid the agreement across the table. "It was all I could think to do to keep him close."

Crystal cradled her coffee mug in both hands. "You're a good person, Dori Mae." She sipped her coffee. "I've learned a lot from you."

"How's Jimmy Jr. taking all this?"

"Oh, he's been surly, but lately he's started dating a nineteen-year-old. He can pull the wool over her eyes, I guess, and I understand now that's what he needs to bolster his ego. If he marries her, I'll probably have to check her mouth for bubble gum before the ceremony."

Dori laughed. "I hope he finds somebody he can be happy with."

"First he has to be happy with himself. His father's never given him much credit for being capable, and Jimmy always thinks he has to prove himself." She ran a manicured fingernail around the rim of her coffee mug. "I'd always hoped you could help him grow up." She smiled. "Instead, you helped me do that."

Dori reached across to squeeze Crystal's hand. "I have a lot to thank you for. All this business with the lawyers. Tell me the cost and I'll pay half."

Crystal shook her head. "No. Let James pay. He owes you at least that much, although he'll never acknowledge it." She gazed at Dori. "You probably wonder why I stay with him."

"Crystal, that's your business. I—"

"I've asked myself the same thing. The truth is, I'm lazy. I don't want to go through the hassle of divorce and I'd be lonesome living by myself. If I were your age, I might consider starting over, but not at fifty-three."

"I understand. I truly do."

"I'm sure you do. You're a perceptive young woman. And you know—"

The doorbell sounded, and Dori excused herself to answer it. Another package had arrived in the overnight mail from Dallas, and this time it was addressed to her. This package was slimmer than the one Little Jim had received two weeks before. Heart pounding, Dori carried it back to the kitchen.

Crystal glanced up, obviously curious, but she didn't ask any questions.

"Um, it's something from Tanner." Dori laid it on the counter, unopened.

"And you want some privacy before you open it." Crystal pushed back her chair and stood.

"You don't have to leave yet," Dori protested, although Crystal had hit the nail on the head. She was dying to open the package but didn't know how she'd react to whatever was inside. She did want privacy.

"I need to get going, anyway." Crystal picked up the custody agreement. "Thanks for the coffee and the pictures. I'll let you know when the hearing is scheduled." She hesitated and glanced out the window at the children on the swing set.

"Did you want to say goodbye? I can call him in."

"No, actually I . . ." Crystal made an impatient gesture. "Never mind. It's too soon."

"Too soon for what?"

"I was thinking of asking if Little Jim could spend the night, but you probably don't want to do that yet. I wouldn't trust us, if I were in your shoes."

Dori felt a nervous clutching of her stomach at the thought of Little Jim being away from her for the night.

"I'd bring him back first thing in the morning," Crystal said. She looked pathetically eager. "I—I miss him something terrible."

Dori looked into Crystal's eyes and saw only goodwill there. She had to start trusting the Devaneys at some point, because the new agreement would give them the right to have Little Jim every other weekend. She might as well start now. "Sure," she said. "I imagine he'd love to go. Especially if you bake cookies with him."

"That was my plan." Crystal came over and hugged her. When she backed away there were tears in her eyes.

"Thank you. Thank you so much. If you want time to get him ready, I'll come back whenever you say."

Dori figured the longer she had to think about it, the more nervous she'd become. "If you don't mind taking him a little dusty, he can go now."

"Bless you."

"Let's go get him."

AS DORI HAD SUSPECTED, Little Jim was happy to go spend a night with his grandmother, who had become an important person in his life. She'd stood up for his rights, and he trusted her as he might never trust his father and grandfather. Dori was just as glad that her son maintained some suspicion toward those two men. They were unlikely to change much.

Ten minutes later Crystal drove away with Little Jim ensconced in the passenger seat of her blue Cadillac, and Dori went back to the kitchen. She called to cancel the baby-sitter and picked up her package from Tanner.

She stood there holding it for a moment and tried to imagine what he could be sending her. Perhaps it had something to do with the custody case. She'd wondered if his lawyers had kept in touch with the Devaney lawyers and if part of Crystal's efficiency had been prompted by Tanner's lawyers breathing down her neck. Crystal wanted to do the right thing, no doubt, but Dori knew she wouldn't want costly lawsuits any more than James would. Crystal liked her life-style.

So Tanner was probably sending her an update. Something impersonal. Still, her heart raced as she pulled the tab and took out an official-looking document. So she'd been right. A note in Tanner's handwriting was paper-clipped to the first page.

Dear Dori,
This is the best I can do.

Love, Tanner

Kind of an odd thing to say, she thought as she glanced at the first page. Then her eyes widened and she groped for a chair as her knees grew weak. She started reading, stumbling over all the whereas and wherefore clauses, but getting the central meaning of the document in front of her. She put her head in her hands and tried to steady her breathing.

The papers, when signed, would make her a full partner in Jones Construction.

TANNER HAD PARKED his red Dodge Ram a block away from Dori's house where he could see the overnight mail truck arrive. He noticed Crystal's Cadillac was in the driveway. According to reports from his lawyers, Crystal was hurrying the custody case along, both for Little Jim's sake and for her own. She understood, even if her husband did not, that the Devaneys would be sued within an inch of their lives if they didn't move quickly. But he still gave Crystal credit for standing up to her husband on Little Jim's behalf.

After the mail truck left, Tanner wondered if Dori was reading the document he'd sent, or if she'd put it aside because Crystal was still there. A short while later, Crystal came out with her grandson and they both climbed into the Cadillac. Good. Tanner had asked Crystal to spirit Little Jim away if possible, but he hadn't been sure Dori would agree to it. Having Dori all to himself, even for a short while, would improve his chances a thousand percent. There were some methods of persuasion he wouldn't be able to employ with her son around.

He glanced at his watch and decided to give her fifteen minutes to read the document. Franklin had stammered like a schoolboy when Tanner had announced what he wanted in the way of a partnership contract. When Franklin had recovered from his shock, he'd mentioned that this was a damned far cry from the prenuptial agreement Tanner had asked him to prepare for any prospective bride. Franklin had repeated all Tanner's lectures about why he didn't want to have partners, let alone a wife who could ruin his business with one nasty divorce. And now Tanner wanted to make this woman a full partner, give her fifty percent of all he owned, before she'd even agreed to marry him? Franklin had suggested that perhaps Tanner needed a checkup. He seemed to be having a breakdown of some sort.

Franklin had been more right than he knew, Tanner thought as he watched the front of Dori's house. He was having a breakdown, and Dori Mae Fitzgerald was the only one who could put the pieces back together. He'd gone into this venture wanting exactly what she'd accused him of wanting, a little wife—somebody who wouldn't threaten his precious business or interfere too much in his schedule, somebody who would adore him and tell him how wonderful he was without making demands of her own.

And then he'd met Dori, who insisted on being a whole person and not an adjunct to some important man. She wanted equal footing, and this was the only way, short of bankrupting himself, that he could think of giving it to her. It was no paper title; the document specified that she'd have definite duties as his partner, including attending meetings and making recommendations on all projects. She'd have a lot to learn, but a woman of her intelligence would have no problem adjusting. She probably knew more than she realized. After all, she'd grown up around a father who was in construction.

Yet he could imagine her turning him down flat. He could imagine it in painful detail. That's why he wouldn't give her too much time before he moved in.

After fourteen minutes he started up the truck. As he pulled into her driveway, he couldn't remember being this nervous in his entire life. But then, nothing had ever been as important as her answer. He strode to the front door with more confidence than he felt and pressed the bell.

DORI WAS STILL STARING at the contract when the doorbell rang. She glanced up at the calendar again. Definitely the ninth of the month. And Tanner had been known to use her magic number to his advantage. Her heart thudding, she left the contract lying on the table and walked to the door.

Although she'd expected to see Tanner on the other side of it, the breath still whooshed out of her when she saw that he was really, truly there. All signs of his injuries were gone, and his eyes shone clear and blue, and filled with love for her. It took all her resolve not to fling herself into his arms. But she still had to decide what to do, and the decision was so very important.

"May I come in?" he asked gently.

"Of course." She stepped aside and he came through the door, bringing with him a remembered scent, a remembered way of moving that turned her insides to jelly. Before she closed the door she got a glimpse of the truck he'd driven this time. It was a far cry from the battered heap he'd arrived in several weeks ago.

But Tanner looked the same. His jeans still hugged his hips and reflected many washings, and his Western shirt was as faded as the one he'd worn when she'd first glimpsed him in the Double Nickel Café.

She licked her dry lips and gestured toward the couch. "Would you like to sit down?"

"Sure." He ambled over to the couch, but she noticed the tense line of his shoulders and decided he wasn't as nonchalant as he looked.

"Coffee?"

"No, thanks." He lifted off his black Stetson and laid it on the arm of the couch.

Dori took the easy chair opposite him, so that the coffee table separated them. Her gaze lingered on his face as she mentally retraced the sweep of his cheekbones, the curve of his jaw, the laugh lines bracketing his mouth and the faint horizontal lines across his forehead where he'd wrinkled his brow with worry. She'd probably given him a fair share of that worry lately. "Little Jim really loves having his White Ranger back. He thinks you found the original one. I didn't have the heart to tell him his daddy destroyed it."

Tanner nodded. "I figured that had happened. That's why I took all the tags off the new one." He smiled, and Dori's heart swelled with longing. "The thank-you note he dictated to you was great. And the drawing."

"I want him to learn good manners. A gift deserves a thank-you."

He leaned forward. "Just to clear the record, what I sent you today wasn't a gift."

Her breathing grew shallow at the fierce light in his eyes. "Then what was it?"

"A business deal. I've discovered I can't run my company without you."

She gripped the arms of the easy chair. "That's ridiculous."

"Ask anybody who works for me. I can't concentrate. I waffle on decisions and let details slip through my fingers. I need somebody with a clear head to help me run things."

"You could hire an assistant."

"I don't want an assistant." His gaze was as direct as a laser beam. "I want an equal. Somebody who will tell me to take a long walk off a short pier when necessary. Somebody tough and independent, with a good head on her shoulders. Somebody exactly like you."

"To help you run your business?"

"For starters. If you'll agree to that, I want you to be my wife."

"People buy into businesses, Tanner. They don't just become partners with a stroke of the pen. I wouldn't have any equity in Jones Construction."

"You already own the heart of the man trying to run it now," he said quietly. "How much is that worth?"

"Oh, Tanner..."

"I've listened to all you've said, and you were right. But I've changed. I want what you want. I have plans to create a community near Abilene that takes advantage of the sweep of the plains the way my houses near Dallas make use of the woods and the lakes. You'll help me, because you have a better feel for this land than I do. Your father can help me. Build a life with me, Dori."

Her head was spinning. She didn't want to be lured into the wrong decision, but he was so appealing, sitting there with his earnest expression. She groped for her objections to his plan. "I don't know how to be rich. I tried to fit in with the way the Devaneys did things, and I couldn't. I'm not comfortable with fancy cars and hotel suites where your clothes are laid out for you every day, and—"

"Neither am I. But money can buy other things. A deserted island in the middle of a turquoise sea of warm water." His voice became a caress. "A little hut, with enough provisions flown in to last a week. Soft sand you can sink your bare toes into as you walk in the sunlight, or the moonlight. A place where no one else will bother you." His voice dropped to a murmur. "And no one lays out your clothes, because you don't have to wear any."

Desire stirred, hot and furious, within her. "That sounds sinful."

"There's nothing sinful about it if you're on your honeymoon."

"A deserted island?" She couldn't help it. She pictured them there, playing at being Adam and Eve in the Garden of Eden. "Are you making this up?"

"I flew there last week to scout it out. The temperature is perfect, Dori. We can pick fruit from the trees, cook on an outdoor grill, make love under the stars. The world will disappear and there will only be the two of us. I reserved the island for a week beginning the ninth of December."

"Tanner! That was taking a big chance."

"No, it wasn't." He rose from the couch and came over to kneel by her chair. "Sending you the contract was taking a big chance. I was afraid you might throw it in my face."

"I couldn't throw anything into such a dear face." She smoothed her palm over his cheek, and he caught her hand and turned his head to kiss it.

He closed his eyes and took a shaky breath. "Marry me, Dori." He looked up into her eyes. "My life isn't worth a plugged nickel without you in it."

"You planned this, on the ninth of the month," she murmured, cradling his head between her hands. "That was very devious of you, Tanner."

"I wanted every advantage I could get. I thought of coming into the café at nine o'clock tonight, which would be a nice touch, but I couldn't wait that long."

"Speaking of that, I have to go to work soon."

He stood and drew her to her feet. "Alice said she'd fill in."

"You talked to Alice?" Then a suspicion entered her mind. "And Crystal?"

"The whole town knows I'm here." He brought her in tight against his aroused body. "And they're all on my side."

"You're a sweet-talkin' man, Tanner Jones."

"Am I sweet enough?"

"Yes," she whispered just before she kissed him with all the love in her heart.

Epilogue

WARM WAVES SWISHED like lace ruffles on the hem of a turquoise negligee. A few feet up the sloping beach, two towels lay spread on sand the color and consistency of light brown sugar. For the first time in her life Dori had an all-over tan.

She lay on her stomach, a briefcase beside her and corporate reports spread across the top of the towel. Tanner reached over and ran a finger down her spine. She brushed him away. "You know I can't concentrate when you do that."

"Depends on what you're trying to concentrate on."

She pulled her sunglasses down her nose and glanced at him over the top of them. "If I'm half owner of this business, I want to understand everything about it."

Tanner put his sunglasses aside and moved over to her towel. "I built the business. I think your best strategy would be to study me."

"I just bet you do." She laughed as he swept the documents out of the way and took her into his arms. His skin was warm from the sun and he was scented with coconut suntan lotion.

"I should never have let you bring that briefcase." He took off her sunglasses and nuzzled her neck before placing an exploratory hand between her thighs.

"You said I could bring reading material." But she'd already lost interest in the reports. The tropical sun kept her skin and blood permanently heated to the temperature of lovemaking. All Tanner had to do was touch her and she became as pliable as a mound of sand.

"I should have been more specific." He fondled her breast with lazy strokes of his palm. "I thought women brought sexy novels to the beach."

"There you go, generalizing again."

"I really have to learn not to do that." He licked the space between her breasts. "You taste like coconut."

"So do you."

"Having a good time?"

"Tanner, this is better than winning the lottery."

"I should hope so. I—"

"That's it!" She sat up, toppling him off the towel.

"I don't think so, Dori. I'm good, but not that good. I barely touched you, and I don't think you're so responsive that you—"

"No, I mean, that's how I'll pay you for my share of the business!"

"You've lost me."

She laughed as she leaned down to give him a resounding kiss. "I nearly forgot, with all that's been going on. But you see, I'll win the lottery in 1999. I have it all worked out. I'll buy the ticket at nine in the morning, on September ninth." She threw her hands into the air. "And I'll be rich! I can pay you for my share in only three years!"

Tanner chuckled and drew her gently back down to the towel. "Thank goodness for that. I was worried about it."

"Well, worry no longer. I will soon be a full partner in all ways."

"I have no doubt." Tanner moved over her. "But right now, there's only one aspect of this partnership I'm concerned about, Mrs. Jones." And with that he solidified their contract in the way Dori had found was the most gratifying of all.

COMING NEXT MONTH

#601 THE HIGHWAYMAN Madeline Harper
Rogues, Book 5

When a quiet drive in the New York countryside turned into a time-travel trip from hell, Olivia Johnson *knew* her life would never be the same. Not only did she find herself in 1796 England, but worse, she'd fallen madly in love with a notorious highwayman—a highwayman who would hang before the year was out....

#602 FOR THE THRILL OF IT Patricia Ryan

Thrill seeker and confirmed bachelor Clay Granger was tired of dodging matrimony. When his best friend, Izzy, revealed she was pregnant and deserted by another man, he saw a solution to *both* their problems. It might even be an adventure! But a platonic marriage wasn't easy when neither one really wanted it that way....

#603 MIDNIGHT TRAIN FROM GEORGIA Glenda Sanders
The Wrong Bed

Erica O'Leary wasn't expecting her trip to Baltimore to be a picnic. But when a rowdy group of Irish-American attorneys decided to continue their St. Patrick's Day partying on the train, it couldn't get any worse. At least she had a sleeping car! But when Erica woke up beside a gorgeous stranger, she knew her nightmare—or fantasy—had just begun!

#604 THE TEXAN TAKES A WIFE Kristine Rolofson
Mail Order Men

Ben Bradley wasn't thrilled when his matchmaking mother placed a personal ad in *Texas Men* magazine—for *him*. And when women started showing up at the ranch in droves, he'd had it! Little wonder he sought refuge with his sympathetic yet surprisingly sexy housekeeper....

MILLION DOLLAR SWEEPSTAKES
AND
EXTRA BONUS PRIZE DRAWING

No purchase necessary. To enter the sweepstakes, follow the directions published and complete and mail your Official Entry Form. If your Official Entry Form is missing, or you wish to obtain an additional one (limit: one Official Entry Form per request, one request per outer mailing envelope) send a separate, stamped, self-addressed #10 envelope (4 1/8" X 9 1/2") via first class mail to: Million Dollar Sweepstakes and Extra Bonus Prize Drawing Entry Form, P.O. Box 1867, Buffalo, NY 14269-1867. Request must be received no later than January 15, 1998. For eligibility into the sweepstakes, entries must be received no later than March 31,1998. No liability is assumed for printing errors, lost, late, non-delivered or misdirected entries. Odds of winning are determined by the number of eligible entries distributed and received.

Sweepstakes open to residents of the U.S. (except Puerto Rico), Canada and Europe who are 18 years of age or older. All applicable laws and regulations apply. Sweepstakes offer void wherever prohibited by law. Values of all prizes are in U.S. currency. This sweepstakes is presented by Torstar Corp., its subsidiaries and affiliates, in conjunction with book, merchandise and/or product offerings. For a copy of the Official Rules governing this sweepstakes, send a self-addressed, stamped envelope (WA residents need not affix return postage) to: MILLION DOLLAR SWEEP-STAKES AND EXTRA BONUS PRIZE DRAWING Rules, P.O. Box 4470, Blair, NE 68009-4470, USA.

FAST CASH 4032 DRAW RULES
NO PURCHASE OR OBLIGATION NECESSARY

Fifty prizes of $50 each will be awarded in random drawings to be conducted no later than 11/28/96 from amongst all eligible responses to this prize offer received as of 10/15/96. To enter, follow directions, affix 1st-class postage and mail OR write Fast Cash 4032 on a 3" x 5" card along with your name and address and mail that card to: Harlequin's Fast Cash 4032 Draw, P.O. Box 1395, Buffalo, NY 14240-1395 OR P.O. Box 618, Fort Erie, Ontario L2A 5X3. (Limit: one entry per outer envelope; all entries must be sent via 1st-class mail.) Limit: one prize per household. Odds of winning are determined by the number of eligible responses received. Offer is open only to residents of the U.S. (except Puerto Rico) and Canada and is void wherever prohibited by law. All applicable laws and regulations apply. Any litigation within the province of Quebec respecting the conduct and awarding of a prize in this sweepstakes may be submitted to the Régie des alcools, des courses et des jeux. In order for a Canadian resident to win a prize, that person will be required to correctly answer a time-limited arithmetical skill-testing question to be administered by mail. Names of winners available after 12/28/96 by sending a self-addressed, stamped envelope to: Fast Cash 4032 Draw Winners, P.O. Box 4200, Blair, NE 68009-4200.

Free Gift Offer

With a Free Gift proof-of-purchase
from any Harlequin® book, you can receive
a beautiful cubic zirconia pendant.

This stunning marquise-shaped stone is a genuine cubic
zirconia—accented by an 18" gold tone necklace.
(Approximate retail value $19.95)

Send for yours today...
compliments of HARLEQUIN®

To receive your free gift, a cubic zirconia pendant, send us one original proof-of-purchase, photocopies not accepted, from the back of any Harlequin Romance®, Harlequin Presents®, Harlequin Temptation®, Harlequin Superromance®, Harlequin Intrigue®, Harlequin American Romance®, or Harlequin Historicals® title available in August, September or October at your favorite retail outlet, together with the Free Gift Certificate, plus a check or money order for $1.65 U.S./$2.15 CAN. (do not send cash) to cover postage and handling, payable to Harlequin Free Gift Offer. We will send you the specified gift. Allow 6 to 8 weeks for delivery. Offer good until October 31, 1996 or while quantities last. Offer valid in the U.S. and Canada only.

Free Gift Certificate

Name: _____

Address: _____

City: _____ State/Province: _____ Zip/Postal Code: _____

Mail this certificate, one proof-of-purchase and a check or money order for postage and handling to: HARLEQUIN FREE GIFT OFFER 1996. In the U.S.: 3010 Walden Avenue, P.O. Box 9071, Buffalo NY 14269-9057. In Canada: P.O. Box 604, Fort Erie, Ontario L2Z 5X3.

FREE GIFT OFFER   084-KMF

ONE PROOF-OF-PURCHASE
To collect your fabulous FREE GIFT, a cubic zirconia pendant, you must include this original proof-of-purchase for each gift with the properly completed Free Gift Certificate.

084-KMF

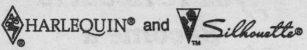

HARLEQUIN® and Silhouette®

are proud to present...

HERE COME THE GROOMS™

Four marriage-minded stories written by top
Harlequin and Silhouette authors!

Next month, you'll find:

A Practical Marriage	by Dallas Schulze
Marry Sunshine	by Anne McAllister
The Cowboy and the Chauffeur	by Elizabeth August
McConnell's Bride	by Naomi Horton

ADDED BONUS! In every edition of
Here Come the Grooms you'll find $5.00 worth
of coupons good for Harlequin and Silhouette
products.

On sale at your favorite Harlequin and Silhouette
retail outlet.

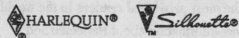
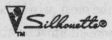

HARLEQUIN® Silhouette®

HCTG896

Look us up on-line at: http://www.romance.net

You're About to Become a *Privileged Woman*

Reap the rewards of fabulous free gifts and benefits with proofs-of-purchase from Harlequin and Silhouette books

Pages & Privileges™

It's our way of thanking you for buying our books at your favorite retail stores.

PROOF OF PURCHASE
HT-PP160
Offer expires October 31, 1996

**Harlequin and Silhouette—
the most privileged readers in the world!**

For more information about Harlequin and Silhouette's PAGES & PRIVILEGES program call the Pages & Privileges Benefits Desk: 1-503-794-2499

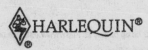

HARLEQUIN®

HT-PP160